Royal Christma

Seattle

A very royal Christmas surprise awaits…

As trees go up, snow begins to fall, lights begin to sparkle and gifts are wrapped, the esteemed Seattle General Hospital emergency room team prepares for a festive season they won't soon forget!

Head ER doc Domenico di Rossi has long kept his identity as Crown Prince of Isola Verde a secret, so when his father is admitted to the ER, chaos erupts and unexpected Christmas miracles are set in motion for everyone in the hospital. Now, with lives on the line, secrets to hide, a throne to be claimed, and hearts to win and lose, it's clear that this Christmas will be the most dramatic yet for the team at Seattle General Hospital!

Available now:

Falling for the Secret Prince
by Alison Roberts

Neurosurgeon's Christmas to Remember
by Traci Douglass

And coming soon:

The Bodyguard's Christmas Proposal
by Charlotte Hawkes

The Princess's Christmas Baby
by Louisa George

Dear Reader,

Welcome to book two of the Royal Christmas at Seattle General series. In my story, I'll introduce you to world-renowned neurosurgeon Dr. Max Granger and the hospital's new PR director, Ayanna Franklin, both of whom are no-nonsense type A personalities who think they have no time for the holidays. But fate—and a well-timed viewing of a classic Christmas film—has other ideas.

Unfortunately, the season can also be hard for many people, bringing up memories of the past and fears for the future. This is also the case for Max and Ayanna, and they must work through their feelings and learn to let go in order to reach their happily-ever-after. Along the way are lots of laughs, a few tears and plenty of family foibles. Basically, just like real life. LOL.

I hope you fall in love with this story as much as I did while writing it. And I wish you and yours a most blessed, magical, and marvelous holiday season and a wonderful New Year!

Until next time, happy reading!

Traci

NEUROSURGEON'S CHRISTMAS TO REMEMBER

—

TRACI DOUGLASS

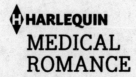

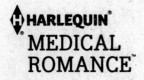

HARLEQUIN®
MEDICAL
ROMANCE™

Recycling programs
for this product may
not exist in your area.

ISBN-13: 978-1-335-14974-9

Neurosurgeon's Christmas to Remember

Harlequin Enterprises ULC
22 Adelaide St. West, 40th Floor
Toronto, Ontario M5H 4E3, Canada
www.Harlequin.com

Printed in U.S.A.

Traci Douglass is a *USA TODAY* bestselling author of contemporary and paranormal romance. Her stories feature sizzling heroes full of dark humor, quick wit and major attitude, and heroines who are smart, tenacious and always give as good as they get. She holds an MFA in Writing Popular Fiction from Seton Hill University, and she loves animals, chocolate, coffee, hot British actors and sarcasm—not necessarily in that order.

Books by Traci Douglass

Harlequin Medical Romance

One Night with the Army Doc
Finding Her Forever Family
A Mistletoe Kiss for the Single Dad
A Weekend with Her Fake Fiancé
Their Hot Hawaiian Fling

Visit the Author Profile page at Harlequin.com.

To all the health-care angels out there who rush in where fools fear to tread.

Thank you for all you do to keep us safe!

**Praise for
Traci Douglass**

"*A Weekend with Her Fake Fiancé* gave me all the feels! I have come to love the Medical Romance books by this author and this one was so fantastic! The writing in this book is excellent with well fleshed out characters and a fun, passionate story line."

—*Goodreads*

CHAPTER ONE

CONTROLLED CHAOS.

Two words that described both the scene playing out before Ayanna Franklin's eyes and her stressful first day as Head of Public Relations for Seattle General Hospital.

Of course, she'd expected the mess she'd walked into first thing this morning. After all, she'd been hired last minute to replace the outgoing director, who'd resigned abruptly to deal with a personal crisis and left Ayanna to deal with preparing for the hospital's huge Christmas ball in a few weeks. Because of said personal crisis, her predecessor had dropped the ball on pretty much everything, meaning Ayanna had to somehow organize the biggest fundraiser event of the year with a limited budget and even more limited time.

What she hadn't expected was the text she'd received from the head nurse in the ER, telling her that not only had one of the hospital's high-profile patients arrived in Seattle three weeks early without warning, he'd also been involved in a serious car accident. The patient was currently in the ER, badly injured and unconscious, and basically all hell had broken loose. If Ayanna didn't stay on top of her part in it, the whole situation had the potential to explode into an enormous catastrophe.

Okay. Calm down. You've got this.

Handling problems was her specialty. Growing up with five younger siblings, all of whom she'd had to keep under her watchful eye as babysitter while her busy parents had worked during their childhood, had prepared Ayanna for anything.

Well, almost anything…

After a deep breath to steady her raging pulse, Ayanna headed through the automatic sliding doors into a cacophony of doctors, nurses, gurneys, and patients, making a beeline for the main workstation hub at the center of it all. Most of the staff here she'd met only briefly, but in her peripheral vision she spotted a few familiar faces—Emelia Featherstone, Head of Orthopedics, and Lucas Beaufort, one of the ER doctors. She'd met them both on a tour of the facility earlier in the week. Now they were both

working on Seattle General's VIP patient—
Roberto Baresi, King of Isola Verde. No one
seemed to know why the man had arrived
early and, based on the King's unresponsive-
ness despite the doctors' repeated attempts
to awaken him, it didn't look like they'd find
out anytime soon.

Blood stained the sheet covering the King's
legs and though the sight might've turned
some people's stomachs, Ayanna wasn't
squeamish. Between her younger siblings'
minor scraped knees from bike accidents to
more major broken bones from falling out of
trees or mishaps at Little League practice,
she'd basically seen and heard it all. Plus,
their mother was a retired nurse.

She sidestepped another gurney rushing in
through the ambulance bay doors on her way
to the central workstation. This new patient
was a woman, her dark curly hair and features similar enough to the King's to mark
her as Giada Baresi, Princess of Isola Verde,
Roberto's daughter. Both of them had been
mentioned in the brief she'd received from
Dr. Dominic di Rossi this morning. The
public relations firms she'd worked for had
always made dossiers for visits by their high-
profile clients to cover things like security
and public relations protocol, staff confiden-

tiality, etc., so that was nothing new either. The only differences at Seattle General now were the confidentiality of the medical setting and the fact these people were royalty, not just CEOs or celebrities.

Nearby stood Dr. di Rossi himself, looking strangely pale as he stared at their unconscious patient. He glanced up then and caught Ayanna's eye then headed in her direction.

"Good thing you're here," the head nurse said, diverting Ayanna's attention away from Dr. di Rossi's approach. The woman gestured impatiently from behind the desk toward Ayanna, beckoning her over. "This place is a zoo already."

Ayanna focused on her part here and not the life or death situations playing out around her. It was her duty to keep the King and this accident out of the press, no matter how unexpected his arrival, and she planned to do just that. Ayanna hated failing, so she didn't. At least professionally. In her personal life, though? That was another story.

Shaking off those errant thoughts, she glanced over at Dr. di Rossi, who was still weaving his way toward her through gurneys and staff, then looked back at the nurse. "Have there been any calls from reporters?"

"Not yet." The nurse stepped closer to

allow a crash cart to pass behind her. "But the local news teams have scanners and they'd have picked up the 911 dispatcher's call to the ambulance and police."

"Right." Ayanna's stomach lurched and she swallowed hard against her dry throat, a surge of adrenaline prepping her for proverbial battle. Okay. First priority—keep the press off the scent of the King's accident until she had a better idea of how this would all play out. "If anyone from the media calls, refer them to my office."

"Will do." The nurse nodded. "I also contacted the neurosurgeon, per Dr. di Rossi's protocol. He's left his conference in Vancouver and is flying in now."

"Perfect." Among her other duties, Ayanna had been assigned to retrieve said neurosurgeon, Dr. Max Granger, from the airport before the King's scheduled brain surgery on December fifteenth, still several weeks away. Now, with the accident, he'd be arriving today and so she pulled up the calendar on her phone to try to work him into her already overflowing schedule. "What time is he landing?"

"About an hour from now," the nurse said, then rattled off the flight info.

"Got it." Ayanna typed all the details into

her phone then glanced over at the King again. Her heart went out to the man and his daughter. They were injured and in a foreign country. It must be terrifying, royalty or not. Plus, with it being so near the holidays, that would make things even more difficult. "Is he doing all right?"

"The King's holding his own. For now." The nurse started around the desk to help another patient then said to Ayanna over her shoulder, "I'll text you if anything changes."

"Thanks." Ayanna slid her phone back into the pocket of her blazer just as Dr. di Rossi reached her. Given his worried expression, he could probably use a moment of quiet, and her caretaker instincts took over as she led the man across the hall to a small private conference room. The door closed, shutting out the barrage of noise behind them, and Ayanna relaxed her tense shoulders a bit. "We've got this covered. Nobody knows that the royal family is here. It's still a secret, as originally planned, and all hospital staff are under strict instructions not to talk about their identities, as per the King's demand."

Dr. di Rossi scrubbed a hand over his face. "Why are they here so early? It's three weeks until his scheduled surgery."

"I don't know. Perhaps he wanted to settle

in," Ayanna speculated. "To feel comfortable in the place he's going to be recuperating?"

He shook his head, frowning. Maybe she was wrong. Honestly, she had no idea what royalty normally did with their lives.

"At least we already had all the plans in place. I've contacted his neurosurgeon as well. Max Granger? He was attending a conference in Vancouver but he's already on his way back. He was very concerned to hear that the King may have a head injury. I'm going to collect him at the airport and bring him here."

"Good. Thank you, Ms. Franklin. I need to get back out there now and see what's happening. Excuse me." Dr. di Rossi gave her a curt nod before exiting.

Alone again, Ayanna waited a few moments before opening the door, the scent of antiseptic and bleach stinging her nose. Her high heels clacked on the shiny linoleum floor as she hurried out of the ER and headed back toward her office.

At least I'll get my exercise, working here.

As she walked, Ayanna shoved aside the fatigue threatening to overwhelm her. She thrived on a challenge. The busier she was, the better. It was one reason she was so good at her job. And probably another mark against her in the romance department. At least that was what her ex, Will, had said when he'd broken off their engagement and left Ayanna for her best friend six months ago.

"Maybe if you paid as much attention to me as you do your career, I wouldn't have cheated."

Will's words still haunted her, usually when she was tired or at night when she was alone. As though his sleeping with her best friend could ever be Ayanna's fault.

Honestly, Ayanna had thought she'd done everything right with Will, and that was the problem. She couldn't trust herself any more, or her emotions. And without her instincts to rely on where her heart was concerned, she tended to shut anyone other than her family out just to be safe. She never wanted to go through having her heart broken again and didn't plan on opening herself up like that again for a very long time, if ever.

Ayanna shook off the lingering ache of loneliness in her chest. Will was a disloyal idiot and she was better off without him. The only person responsible for his actions was him. He'd known what her crazy schedule was like before they'd become involved. For him to throw it in her face like that as an excuse for his deplorable behavior was non-sense.

Maybe if she repeated that to herself enough times, she'd finally believe it.

She gave herself a mental shake. No time to dwell on the past. There was too much to do today, starting with prioritizing her current workload now that she had to include a trip to the airport to pick up Dr. Granger.

An image of the stacks of files waiting for her to sort through for the upcoming annual charity Christmas ball put on by Seattle General flashed in her head. This year it was being held at the luxurious four-diamond Polar Club Hotel. The place was an historic treasure in the Pacific Northwest and at least her predecessor had managed to reserve the grand ballroom before their swift departure. The locale gave Ayanna a good canvas to work with, but she had less than a month until the event and the menu and décor were still up in the air, not to mention the musicians. It was a lot to get done in a short amount of time. And with her staff tied up trying to prevent the information about the King's accident from getting out now, they wouldn't be much help either.

But somehow it would all work out. Because the alternative wasn't an option.

Besides, she'd handled worse situations in her days in the PR trenches. In fact, her ability to think on her feet was what had landed her on the list of "Top PR Professionals Under Forty", according to the *Washington Post*. She worked hard and played harder.

Or not at all.

Restless, Ayanna boarded an elevator to her office on the fourth floor. The car jolted upward, and she pulled out her phone again to check her app that was tracking Dr. Granger's flight in real time. On a good day, it took twenty minutes to get to the airport from Seattle General, but with Thanksgiving less than a week away, the city was more packed than usual with tourists. She'd grab her purse and leave now, just to make sure she arrived in plenty of time. The last thing she needed today were more unexpected issues because she somehow missed picking up the King's neurosurgeon.

"Please place your trays in the upright and secure position as we prepare for landing. Thank you." The pilot's voice crackled over the PA system as the "Seatbelt Fastened" signs were illuminated overhead. Dr. Max Granger shut down his laptop and stared out the window at the city below. Afternoon sunlight glinted off the Space Needle in the distance, but he had little time to appreciate the beauty of Seattle and even less inclination.

Since his wife's death two years previously, Max preferred to stay busy. Busy and famous, apparently, if those ridiculous TV tabloid shows that had recently dubbed him the "Brain Surgeon to the Stars" were believed. He sighed and shifted in his seat. Yes, many of his patients were celebrities and dignitaries, including the patient he was flying in to see now—King Roberto Baresi of Isolde Verde—but that was because he was a world-renowned neurosurgeon at the pinnacle of his profession. He was the best at what he did. His upbringing had ensured it. The fact his late parents would've been proud of all he'd accomplished brought him little joy, though. He could count on two hands the number of times they'd spent any quality time with him as he'd been growing up.

Greatness comes at a price.

That had been the motto his parents had taught him as a child and their rationale for leaving him behind with nannies expected to raise him to adulthood. For a long time Max had bought it too. At least until he'd met his late wife, Laura.

Familiar loneliness weighed him down. Two years was a long time to be alone.

But now wasn't the time to get bogged down in the past or his emotions. He had a case to prepare for, one that had just become far more complicated due to the King's accident. Originally, the King's tumor hadn't been a cause for immediate surgical intervention. Meningiomas were generally slow growing and benign. The only real concerning factor had been its location near the sagittal sinus, which—if infiltrated by the tumor—could jeopardize blood flow through the major vein running across the top of the brain. Max had been keeping tabs on his patient through CT scans and had planned to go ahead with a scheduled procedure to remove the meningioma on December fifteenth, still almost a month away.

The accident today, however, had changed those plans. According to the latest update he'd received from the ER staff, his patient's current Glasgow Coma Score was seven. The King had no visual or verbal responses but did show purposeful movement to painful stimuli. An emergency scan of his brain had shown a temporal bleed into the epidural space and Max suspected a hematoma. Given the man's age and the fact the King already had slightly increased intracranial pressure due to his tumor, time was of the essence to restore normal blood flow and avoid permanent damage to the tissues.

The sooner Max got off this plane and to Seattle General, the sooner he could prep for surgery.

"Happy Holidays," a passing flight attendant said, handing him a Santa pin.

He took it from the guy and stuffed it in his pocket without looking at it. He didn't have the time for Christmas cheer. He didn't celebrate the holidays anyway. Not since losing Laura.

His ears popped as the plane descended and his memories returned against his wishes. The irony of his own wife dying of an aneurysm wasn't lost on Max. Rationally, he knew there was little chance anyone could have known of the existence of the weakened blood vessel in Laura's brain. But the knowledge did little to relieve the remorse of not being there for her, the one patient he should have tried his hardest to save.

Now he lived alone. Alone was better anyway. He was too busy for a relationship. Between his speaking engagements and seminars and patients, Max couldn't remember the last time he'd spent more than one night in his apartment back in New York.

The tires jolted on the runway and he rubbed his palm down the leg of his trousers. As the plane taxied toward the gate, Max gathered his carry-on from the overhead bin then checked his phone again for any new updates on the King's condition. Nothing yet.

Finally, the attendant opened the door and Max pushed out of first class. Footsteps pounding up the rampway, he emerged into the busy gate at Seattle-Tacoma International Airport and looked around for the person the hospital had sent to pick him up. Unfortunately, no one made eye contact with him except a perky guy dressed as an elf. Definitely not who he was looking for. They were supposed to have a sign with his name on it for identification. But none of the signs he could see said Max Granger.

Dammit.

Overhead, an announcement proclaimed Santa's helicopter would land soon and North Pole Village was opening in the gallery at the end of Concourse B. Max glanced up at the sign hanging above the walkway and dread welled inside him. Sure enough, he was smack dab at the epicenter of what would soon be a madhouse of kids and parents rushing to see the big man in red.

Guess that explained the elf.

Soon families converged, milling about the area with luggage and children in tow, the little ones clamoring to visit Saint Nick. To add insult to injury, peppy Christmas tunes drifted down from the speaker system, and Max felt more Grinch-like by the second.

Why can't the holidays get out of my way already?

He didn't have time for this. Pulse thudding, he battled his way through the crowds toward the glowing exit sign, switching into strict surgeon mode and turning the invisible dial on his inner turmoil down to zero before firing off a quick text to let the ER staff know his ride hadn't arrived and that he was getting a taxi to the hospital.

He'd failed once to save someone important because of a late arrival. He refused to do so again.

CHAPTER TWO

"SANTA AND MS. CLAUS are landing now, kids! Be sure to get in line!"

Ayanna stared at the increasing mob of people between her and the gate ahead with growing dread. Traffic had been even worse than she'd expected and she'd arrived twenty minutes late. Then she'd had to find a spot in the garage because she hadn't had time to pre-book and she'd ended up far away from the terminal. She'd raced down here as fast as her high heels would allow, but Dr. Granger's plane had already landed and the passengers had disembarked.

Dealing with Santa's arrival on top of everything else was the last straw. It was like some bizarre comedy movie, except none of this was funny. Not to her.

Her phone buzzed with an update from the ER. The King's condition had not improved, and Dr. Granger was needed onsite stat. After trying to cut through the throngs of people ahead of her with little luck, Ayanna finally managed to flag down a ticketing agent. "Can you page someone for me, please? It's an emergency."

"Sorry, ma'am. You'll need to go to Customer Service." The woman pointed back toward the direction Ayanna had come.

Great.

Staying one step ahead was what she normally did best, but today it seemed she'd fallen ten steps behind. Heart hammering against her ribcage, Ayanna slipped out of the line she was in and headed back the way she'd come. She needed to find Dr. Granger and get him to Seattle General. She could stew over the rest of this mess later, once this awful day was over.

Dodging passengers and their rolling suitcases while Bing Crosby crooned "White Christmas," she stood in yet another line behind a woman with a stroller and three small kids. Normally Ayanna loved Christmas, but right now she felt decidedly unjolly.

After a small eternity, she finally reached the counter. "I need to page someone, please."

"Name?" the service agent asked.

Ayanna's phone buzzed in her hand and she looked down to see another message from the ER.

Neurosurgeon on the way in a taxi. Where are you?

"Ma'am?" the customer service rep asked again. "What's the name of the party you're looking for?"

Damn.

She buzzed with an odd mix of relief and irritation. The missing surgeon had been found. That was good. But he'd found his own ride instead of waiting for her to pick him up, which meant she'd screwed up one of her first major tasks as PR director. That was bad. "Uh, I'm sorry. He's been located. Thank you."

She moved out of line to send her reply to her staff.

Still at SeaTac. Long story. On my way now.

Her phone buzzed again, but she was already on her way out of the airport, more angry at herself than anyone. She didn't let people down like this.

Will's stupid face flashed in her head again.

"You're always doing stuff for other people, but what about me?"

The last thing she needed in her mind was her ex and his spiteful last words to her. And the fact they held a tiny kernel of truth didn't make her feel any better. Yes, she was a caretaker. Yes, it made her feel worthwhile. That wasn't a bad thing, was it? Helping others was good.

Besides, her can-do attitude was what had had her graduating with an MBA from Washington University at just twenty-four and landing internships and jobs with the best companies and brightest people in the marketing world. Yes, maybe she had neglected her relationship with Will because of work, but that didn't mean he'd been free to sleep with her best friend.

Disappointment squeezed her chest as she exited the terminal and headed for the parking garage. She'd had her problems, but Will wasn't perfect either. Nope. Not at all. And he'd never understood or appreciated how hard she tried to make everyone else's life easier.

She took the elevator up four levels then strode across the pavement toward her car. After tossing her purse on the passenger seat and buckling her seatbelt, she started the engine then pulled out of the lot and merged back into traffic heading toward downtown Seattle, fielding calls through her Bluetooth as she sat in traffic on the I5, heading north.

"Call the Polar Club Hotel," she said, then waited for it to connect.

With the King's original surgery scheduled for a few weeks in the future, the hotel reservations for Dr. Granger's room needed to be changed to accommodate his earlier arrival and she hadn't had time to do it before she'd left the office.

"Thank you for calling. How may I help you?" the clerk said.

"Yes, my name is Ayanna Franklin and I need to modify reservations made on behalf of Seattle General Hospital for Dr. Maxwell Granger. He's arrived in town earlier than expected and will need the room tonight through at least December twenty-fifth, please."

"Of course, Ms. Franklin," the clerk said, his tone solicitous over the sound of clacking computer keys. "Yes, I've pulled that reservation up. A single room with a king-sized bed."

"Yes."

"Unfortunately, however, with the holidays I'm afraid we're completely booked."

Crap. Could nothing go right today?

Ayanna signaled and changed lanes, then slowed for more stopped vehicles. In the distance, sunlight glinted off the Seattle skyline, but her usual joy at seeing her beloved hometown was dimmed. "What about another room type?"

The clerk typed again. "No. I'm sorry. It looks like we're full up through Christmas. Unless…" Ayanna held her breath as the clerk trailed off, tapping furiously on his keyboard.

One of her greatest strengths was coming up with creative solutions to seemingly insurmountable problems. She could try another hotel, but if the Polar Club was full up, chances were good they all were. Maybe Dr. Granger could stay with her? But, no, that wouldn't work either. Her apartment was too small and they were getting ready to do some electrical work on her place anyway, which meant she was going to have to find a place to stay for a few weeks herself. Perhaps temporary rental then or…

"Ma'am?" the clerk said, breaking into her thoughts. "I do see our Denali Suite is available for the date range you specified. It's a bit larger, though, with two bedrooms, and more expensive than the room originally booked for Dr. Granger."

He rattled off the room price and her mind ticked through the budget set aside for the surgeon's visit. It was more than the hospital had wanted to spend, but if it was the only room available, there wasn't much they could do at this point.

"Fine. We'll take it," she said, staring at the red taillights ahead.

One problem down, a gazillion more to go.

"Marvelous. Anything else I can do for you, Ms. Franklin?"

"No, thank you." She ended the call then exhaled. Right now, she needed to get back to her office and keep an eye on Dr. Granger so he didn't disappear on her again.

She passed a sign for the Redmond exit and the knot in her gut tightened. Her parents lived in Redmond. They'd offered Ayanna her old room to stay in while the work at her apartment was being done, but being home during the holidays was stressful enough without actually living there, what with her five siblings and their significant others filling the space.

She'd find another solution.

I could stay with Dr. Granger. In the extra bedroom.

Wait. What?

Where in the world had *that* come from? She didn't even know the man.

Maybe she'd just sleep in her office. Lord knew, she had enough work to do to get ready for the ball to keep her there round the clock for the next few weeks. She snorted and veered off the highway at her exit, relaxing her death grip on the steering wheel. She had this. Forget the mishap in the airport. From this moment forward, Ayanna was back on her game.

"Could I get some suction here, please?" Max said as he placed the last tiny screw into the bone plate over the temporal region of the King's skull. "And give Radiology thirty minutes' notice also."

"Yes, Doctor," one of the nurses said, while another provided the requested suction to the area he'd indicated.

Max continued suturing in the drain he'd placed. "How are the patient's vitals?"

"Good," the anesthesiologist replied. "Heart rate steady and blood oxygen levels normal."

"Excellent." He handed the last of his instruments to the surgical nurse then stepped away. "And we're done. Thank you, team.

Let's get the patient back to CT to make sure the hematoma's gone."

The nurses took over, cleaning up the area before wheeling the patient away to Radiology. Closure hadn't taken thirty minutes after all, but Max always liked to err on the side of caution. Once the room was empty, he walked out of the OR and into the small room attached to remove his soiled gown and gloves then scrub up post-op.

The King was stable. Tension eased inside him and the tightness in his gut uncoiled. It was probably the fatigue of travel but he felt raw and restless. He didn't do vulnerability well. Never had, really. Not since he'd been eight and his parents had come home unexpectedly from a trip to China. He'd loved his parents so much back then and had been unable to wait to tell them all about the friends he'd made in school and how well he'd done on his math test. Of course, they'd only been interested in whether or not he'd gotten into the fancy boarding school they'd attended. After New Year, they'd gone off to travel the world again and he'd been shipped off to school. From then on out, he'd lived there year round until he'd graduated and headed off to Harvard. At least his parents had shown up to his commencement. Guess he should've been grateful for that.

Max sighed. Maybe it was Christmas that had him on edge. Really, the only time he'd even remotely enjoyed this time of year had been with Laura. She'd loved Christmas and used to decorate their house back in Long Island to within an inch of its life. To this day, he couldn't see reindeer and twinkle lights without thinking of her. Come to think of it, it had been holiday time when he'd last seen his parents too, all those years ago.

He finished washing his hands and arms before yanking a few paper towels from the dispenser. His shoulders gave a painful twinge and he rolled his neck to release the crick there. Man, what he wouldn't give for a hot shower and a long nap. The clock on the wall showed it was well after midnight and between work and seminars he hadn't slept for more than a few hours at a stretch in days.

Stifling a yawn, he pressed the metal accessibility button on the wall with his hip to open the door then backed out into the hallway, only to collide backend first with a woman.

"Sorry," he said, swiveling fast. "Didn't see you there."

"Unless you've got eyes in the back of your

head, I'd say not," she said, giving him a small smile. "Then again, I swear my mother always seems to know what's going on behind her, so…"

Max stared at the petite black woman with her stylish blue business suit and killer high heels. His first thought was that she was cute. Really cute. In fact, she reminded him of an actress he'd seen in a movie recently during one of his many flights. Same smooth skin. Same bright smile. Same adorable dimples.

Whoa. What?

Max shook his head. He didn't care about her cuteness or her dimples or anything else. That wasn't what he was here for. He was here to work. Period.

Still they stared at each other across the span of a few feet and Max swallowed hard against the unwanted interest clawing inside him. Then his old work ethic intervened, bringing him back to his senses. He had no business noticing anything about this woman, other than the fact she was currently in his way. The King's results from the post-op CT scan should be back soon and he needed to check them. No time to stand here gawking over a beautiful woman with wide brown eyes and a smile that made the dark clouds around him vanish for a moment. Before he could contemplate why, one of the surgical nurses called to him from down the hall.

"Films are ready, Dr. Granger."

"Right." He looked back at the woman who was still standing there with her head tilted and her arms crossed, one brow still raised at him as if he were a naughty schoolboy and not an accomplished brain surgeon. "Excuse me," he said, frowning. "Sorry again."

Instead of leaving her behind, however, the woman followed him to the nurses' station. "I'm sorry too, Dr. Granger, but you're not getting away from me again so easily."

"What?" Baffled, he glanced over at her. "Look, I have a patient to deal with, Miss…?"

"Franklin. And, please, do your work," she said, then pulled out her phone and leaned against the wall behind her. "I'll wait, don't worry."

He glanced around to see if anyone else had noticed this strange conversation, but the nurses were all busy. One of them waved him over to a computer. "Doctor."

Max walked around the desk and took a seat to click through the CT images of the King's brain, irritated with himself for getting distracted. Thankfully, everything looked clear and he nodded at the surgical nurse who'd assisted him in the OR. "Looks good. Thanks for your help on such short notice."

"Thank you, Dr. Granger, for being so appreciative," she said, smiling. "Not everyone is."

"Of course." He let her have her seat back. Nurses were the heart and soul of the hospital and could be a doctor's staunchest ally or his worst nightmare. He preferred the former and always tried to be kind and courteous no matter what the situation. He moved to a private corner of the desk to phone Dr. di Rossi and update him on the King's condition. Max was one of the few people at the hospital who knew that the head of the ER was actually King Roberto's son and therefore Prince of Isolde Verde, heir apparent to the throne. He couldn't treat the King properly without a full and accurate medical and family history. As he spoke in hushed tones to Dr. di Rossi, Max could still feel the weight of Miss Franklin's gaze on the nape of his neck, burning a hole through his skin along with his composure. Annoyed, he rubbed the area, as if that might make her go away. She was persistent. He'd give her that.

Finally, he turned around, determined to put a swift end to this odd encounter. "Look, Miss Franklin," Max said, doing his best to keep the annoyance from his voice and failing miserably, if her flat stare was any indication, "I'm not sure who you are or—"

"I'm the PR Director for this hospital and the woman who was supposed to pick you up at the airport. But you left without me and I've spent the last few hours tracking you down. You've already disrupted my busy schedule enough and I won't let that happen again. So, here are some ground rules going forward," she said, her crisp words scraping against his already overtaxed nervous system.

"Once you're changed, I'm taking you to your hotel for the night. Next, I'll pick you up tomorrow morning and each day following to deliver you here to the hospital to see the King. At the end of the day, I'll take you back to your hotel again. Until the King's case is closed and my office has a firm lid on the press about this accident, we'll be seeing a lot more of each other. Any questions?"

CHAPTER THREE

SEVERAL OF THE nurses cast curious looks in her direction at that statement, and Ayanna could've kicked herself. She hadn't meant to blurt it out like that, but it was too late now. Something about this guy ruffled all her feathers and she didn't like it. Not one bit.

"Yeah, I've got a question." Those icy gray eyes of his lit with cold fire. "Who do I speak with to get off lockdown? I don't need a babysitter. Especially one I don't even know."

"Maybe you should've thought of that before you went rogue at SeaTac." So much for biting her tongue. She crossed her arms and waited for him to walk around the desk, taking a deep breath to get herself under control and avoid drawing any more unwanted attention from the staff, who were now whispering amongst themselves and pointing in Ayanna's direction. Perfect. Add "starting a scandal" to her growing list of first-day accomplishments.

"Rogue?" Dr. Granger scrunched his nose then stalked off toward the staff changing room down the hall, leaving her behind. "My patient needed immediate treatment. There was no time to waste." He stopped halfway down the hall and glanced back at her with a chilly glare. "Pardon me if I happen to care more about people's lives than your precious schedule, Ms. Franklin."

Appalled, Ayanna blinked at him several moments before following him. *Oh. No. He. Didn't.* She was doing her best here. "Excuse me, Dr. Granger, but I do care about people's lives, especially those of Seattle General's high-profile patients whose privacy I've been tasked with protecting. And as for us not knowing each other, that should solve itself as we'll be seeing more of each other on a daily basis." She paused a moment to collect her thoughts and lower her defensiveness below red zone levels. "Look, believe me when I say this isn't my ideal situation either, but until your work here is done, I am your new shadow."

Heat pulsed off her cheeks with each beat of her heart and their gazes remained locked. Standing just a few feet away from him, she couldn't help noticing that he was…well, he was *gorgeous*, darn it. Even with those dark shadows under his eyes. Tall, dark hair, piercing gray-green eyes. Man, oh, man. If this guy wasn't on her naughty list, he'd have been just her type.

Except she wasn't looking. Especially at Dr. Granger.

Besides, Will had been handsome as heck too and look how that had turned out. Not well. Not well at all. Nope. Ayanna didn't care if this man was a gift sent straight from the North Pole, she had enough on her plate to deal with at present without a booty call from Dr. Distraction.

"Again, I don't need a babysitter, Ms. Franklin," he growled as he pushed inside the changing room. "I'm a board-certified neurosurgeon with a world-class client list. I'm perfectly capable of getting around on my own, thank you very much."

"Great," she said, her voice dripping with faux cheerfulness. "Then you should have no problem dealing with me."

Ayanna followed him inside the private staffroom, completely unfazed by his grumpiness. She'd seen far worse from her siblings growing up. This late at night the area was deserted except for them, which was good considering their argument had already drawn more attention than she wanted, but she couldn't seem to help herself. For some reason, this man pushed all her buttons without even trying.

"Also, Dr. di Rossi's orders stated you are to be made available at a moment's notice should the King require your services. The only way I can ensure that, after your disappearing act at the airport, is to keep you under my watch until the King's surgery is complete on the fifteenth. So, the sooner you accept it, the easier it will be for both of us. Now, get changed so we can get you checked into your hotel."

With a low growl he yanked open one of the metal lockers against the wall with a clatter, not looking at her. "First of all, I didn't disappear on you, Ms. Franklin. As I've already explained, the King's condition was critical and required my immediate assistance. I didn't have time to go searching for you. I'd appreciate it if you don't make me repeat that information again." Jaw tight, he picked up a wheeled suitcase nearby and sat it atop the wooden bench in front of a row of lockers against one wall, then clicked it open before tugging off his scrub shirt, leaving him naked from the waist up. "Also, there's no need for you to ferry me around town like a chauffeur. I can make my own way to and from the hospital as needed. I'm a grown man."

Grown man indeed.

Her eyes widened as he rummaged around in his suitcase for a shirt. Flushed and flustered, Ayanna turned away fast but not before she'd gotten a peek at all those rippling muscles and smooth, tanned skin.

Sweet Santa on a sleigh, why is it so hot in here?

She resisted the urge to fan herself and stared at the white wall opposite her instead.

Get a grip, girl. He's just a man.

A man who obviously kept himself in peak physical condition despite his busy schedule.

"Why do you need keep tabs on my every move anyway, Ms. Franklin?" he grumbled from behind her as he changed. She only half listened to him, doing her best not to imagine him stripping off those scrub pants too, and didn't dare turn around for fear of seeing her wicked fantasies realized. Lord, this was ridiculous. Okay, sure. She hadn't been with a man since Will. And, yes, maybe six months of celibacy was too long for a red-blooded woman like her. That had to be the reason why this man was affecting her so strongly, right? Thankfully, his sharp tone jarred her out of the smutty pool she'd fallen into and back to reality. "Please don't tell me you're some kind of control freak."

The label struck a painful chord, reminding her of Will's spiteful attitude toward her work hours. She wasn't a control freak. People depended on her to handle things. It's what she did, who she was.

But she wasn't about to stand here and defend herself to this man who couldn't be bothered to follow the simplest of directions. No. At this point the best thing was to get Dr. Bah Humbug to the hotel and checked in, then part ways for the evening. Maybe after some sleep they could meet again on better terms. She cleared her throat and squared her shoulders. "I'll wait for you outside."

"Sure you don't want to stay and help me tie my shoes?" he called from behind her as she headed for the door. "I might find a way out of here through the ceiling tiles and escape again."

Ayanna couldn't resist glancing back at him then, one hand on the cool metal door handle as she tried to bite back a smile and saw he had regular black pants on and was buttoning up a white dress shirt, tiny splotches of crimson dotting his high cheek-bones.

"I'll take my chances," she said, mimicking his sarcastic tone with one of her own. "Five minutes."

She exited the room head held high, far too aware of the weight of his gaze on her back as she walked out into the brightly lit hallway once more. Her throat felt tight and for some reason that image of his long fingers fastening the front of his shirt was burned into her brain. Those were good hands. Sturdy and strong. Her traitorous mind had her imagining all the things those hands could do to her before she stopped herself.

What is wrong with me?

The cooler air felt good on her heated cheeks. She slumped back against the wall several feet down from the door and closed her eyes, searching in vain for her missing composure. This wasn't like her at all. She was always the go-to gal in a crisis. Yet one encounter with Dr. Granger had thrown her entire ordered world asunder. Well, no more.

Inhaling deeply, Ayanna straightened and smoothed a hand down the front of her cerulean blue pantsuit. She'd bought it last month and had been so excited to wear it for the first time today. The salesgirl had said the color highlighted the pink tones in her complexion and made her skin glow. She could sure as hell use all the shine she could get at the moment.

Fine. Enough. Yes, she and Dr. Granger had gotten off to a rocky start, but they were both professionals and while the current circumstances weren't ideal, they would make the best of them. Starting with reaching an accord before she dropped the man off at his hotel for the night.

Dr. Granger exited the changing room a few moments later, still scowling and muttering under his breath as he made a beeline for the elevators, wheeling his suitcase right past her as if she weren't there. Undeterred, Ayanna quickly caught up with him and waited beside him in front of the gleaming metal doors. He felt big next to her, the heat of him penetrating the sleeve of her jacket as their arms brushed. With that grim set to his lips and the faint lines of tension around his mouth and eyes, his presence screamed alpha male dominance.

To her chagrin, her ovaries gave a tiny squeeze before she put a quick kibosh on that. The last thing she needed was input from her reproductive system.

She'd hoped to have babies with Will, until she'd discovered he was a lying, cheating snake beneath his slick exterior and she knew she could still have kids. She was only thirty-two, for goodness' sake. Now, if she could just ignore that tick-tick-tick of her biological clock and the well-meaning hints her parents kept dropping about grandchildren, she'd be all set.

"We've booked you a suite at the Polar Club," she said, both to distract herself and to break the near-stifling silence that had fallen between them. When he didn't respond, Ayanna side-eyed him from beneath her lashes. "With you arriving earlier than originally planned, I upgraded your accommodations to a suite."

"I'm perfectly fine with a standard room." He exhaled slowly through his nose, as if summoning the last of his patience. Then he shook his head and his broad shoulders relaxed slightly, the corners of his firm lips turning down. "But thank you for making the adjustment."

"You're welcome." Given the reluctance in his voice, she'd bet that concession had cost him a lot. He was tired, that much was plain, given the dark circles beneath his eyes and his slightly rumpled appearance. She was exhausted too. Still, she couldn't help wondering if his prickly demeanor was caused by more than lack of sleep. "And the suite was the only room they had left. All the local hotels are booked solid through the holidays."

The elevator dinged and the doors swished open. Ayanna held them for him while he trundled himself and his suitcase on, then followed him. She pushed the button for the walkway level then stepped back and clasped her hands in front of her, her tote over her shoulder.

As they descended, Dr. Granger's posture remained stiff. "So we're stuck with each other, then?"

"We are." The elevator dinged and the doors opened once more. As they walked, she pointed out different areas of interest to him, including the cafeteria and where his interim office would be located in the neurology department, just down the hall from her own.

Finally, they reached the parking lot across the street where her car was parked. Dr. Granger hadn't said much as they walked and now that she really looked at him again, he seemed almost forlorn without his gruff bravado. It was endearing, in an odd sort of way that pulled at her heartstrings, and before she knew it Ayanna's fixer mode kicked in and an apology fizzed to the tip of her tongue before she could stop it. "We started on the wrong foot earlier at the nurses' station and I'm sorry."

They crossed the street, the late-November air crisp, the starry sky above clear for a change. Weather in Seattle was nothing if not unpredictable at this time of year. When he didn't respond, she continued, feeling the need to make him understand, though she couldn't say exactly why. "I'm under a bit more stress than usual as it's my first day at Seattle General and I apologize if I took some of that out on you. And I don't mean to act like a mother hen, but Dr. di Rossi's orders were clear. My only concern is making sure you get where you need to be as conveniently as possible. I'm here to make your life easier."

He looked over at her, the orange glow from the streetlight above casting deep shadows on his face. For a moment she worried he might argue again, but then he sighed and shook his head. "I'm sorry too. I should've have looked harder for you at the airport, but as I said my patient's condition is my priority, and I needed to get to Seattle General immediately."

After loading his luggage into the back of her vehicle, they headed out of the lot, Ayanna scanning her badge at the exit before turning out onto the street. Trying to fill the conversational void, she asked, "Is this your first visit to the Pacific Northwest, Dr. Granger?"

"No," he said, the dashboard GPS screen highlighting his profile as he stared out of the window beside him. "I was here a few months ago for a seminar on improved accuracy in frameless stereotaxy."

"Oh." Ayanna had no idea what that meant, but now that he was talking again she wanted to keep it going. "Seminars probably don't allow much time to explore your location, though, do they?"

That got her a low grunt in response. After a moment he looked over at her once more. "You should probably call me Max since we'll be seeing more of each other."

She blinked straight ahead. "Okay, Max. And please call me Ayanna."

Minutes later, they pulled up to the curb on Third Avenue in front of the Polar Club and she got out, handing her keys to a waiting valet. After a bellman retrieved Dr. Granger's suitcase, they went inside to check in.

Ayanna had always loved this place. The

lobby looked like something out of a turn-of-the-century gentlemen's club, all dark woods and plush velvet upholstery, with thick oriental rugs under foot and a fire crackling in the fireplace. Golden Christmas lights twinkled from the mantel and a large, plump spruce was decorated in one corner in tasteful shades of gold and green.

Beside her, Max's expression was pleasingly awed. Maybe she'd finally gotten something right with him. The thought she'd made him happy caused an unexpected prickle of satisfaction inside Ayanna before she quickly shoved it aside. This was her job. That's all.

They approached the large, carved wooden reservation desk across from the fireplace and she smiled at the clerk. "Hello, reservation for Dr. Maxwell Granger. I called earlier."

"Ah, yes. Ms. Franklin," the clerk said. "We spoke on the phone."

"Right. Thank you for your help."

"My pleasure," His gaze flicked to Max, who'd moved in beside Ayanna. "Will you be staying in the suite as well, Miss Franklin?"

"No!" they both said in unison, a bit louder than necessary.

Ayanna cleared her throat. "The room belongs to Dr. Granger. He'll be in town for the next few weeks, working on a case."

"Very good." If the clerk thought that statement was odd, he didn't show it. Then again, Ayanna figured he probably got lots of practice hiding his reactions to people's strange arrangements in his job. The clerk printed out the paperwork and Ayanna signed it on behalf of Seattle General then waited while Max got his key card and a map of the hotel. "The elevators are down the hall. Please enjoy your stay with us, Dr. Granger. Happy Holidays."

Max grunted again then started off down the corridor.

"Thank you. Happy Holidays to you too," Ayanna said, before racing off after Max. Whatever the guy had against the season she didn't know, but the idea of finding out why intrigued her far more than it should.

Max set his suitcase against the wall and stared at the spacious suite before him. Floor-to-ceiling windows across one wall led to a large balcony spanning the entire length of the room that showcased spectacular views of downtown Seattle. From the custom wall-paper to the shiny hardwood floors, the room was amazing and held a special touch of Northwest flavor.

"This is even nicer than I expected," Ayanna said, sidling past him into the nicely appointed kitchen area and setting her bag on the counter. The black leather matched her shoes, he noticed. In fact, everything about her appearance was precise and perfectly coordinated, from her silky dark shoulder-length hair to her expertly applied makeup. Based on what he'd seen so far, he'd say Ayanna Franklin left little to chance when it came to her life. Not that he cared. Her life and how she chose to live it were none of his business. He was here to care for the King. That was all.

Ayanna peered inside the empty stainless-steel fridge and the smaller mini-fridge. The latter was brimming with assorted snacks and booze. She peered back at him over her shoulder, her pretty smile expectant, and something coiled tight inside him before he brushed it away. "What do you think?"

"It's fine," he mumbled, scowling down at his shoes. The room was far more than fine, but he likely wouldn't get to enjoy it too much. He was here to work, not to lounge in his luxury accommodation.

Max turned away, but not before he caught

the flicker of hurt in her expression. Guilt pinched his ribcage. Dammit. She'd interpreted his remoteness as rudeness, but it wasn't personal towards her. He didn't allow anyone close these days. The difficulty of his cases required peace, quiet and intense concentration. Distractions could be lethal, so he avoided them at all costs. Yet for some reason Ayanna Franklin seemed to have gotten further under his skin in a few hours than anyone had since his wife's passing.

It was baffling. It was bewildering. It was very bad indeed.

Normally, he tried his best to be cordial to everyone. And while he traveled often for his job, never staying in one place long enough to make real connections, most people liked him. Max Granger, they said, was easy to get along with. A team player. But something about this woman tonight had set his nerves on edge and nothing since had put them right.

She closed the mini-fridge then grabbed her bag off the counter. "Well, Dr. Granger, you look exhausted. If everything is satisfactory here with your room, I'll be going."

A hint of her scent—spice and cloves and a hint of rose—filled the air as she passed him, teasing his senses and driving his awareness of her higher. For a crazy second he was tempted to ask her stay, but why? They were both obviously ruffled and spending more time together wouldn't end this evening any sooner and get him the privacy he craved. So, instead he said, "Yes, if you'll excuse me, I'd like to shower then get some sleep. I'm very tired."

"Great." Ayanna hesitated near the door, watching him across the span of a few feet, her dark eyes wide. She licked her lips and damn if he couldn't stop himself from tracking that tiny movement, his jumbled mind immediately wondering what her mouth would taste like, if those lips felt as soft as they looked, what sounds she might make if he pulled her against him and kissed her…

Whoa. What the—?

Max stepped back and turned away, coughing to relieve the pressure of his heart lodged in his throat. He never acted like this. There was no excuse for his behavior. Not exhaustion. Not unwanted lust.

Confused, he took a step back, then another, until his butt hit the edge of the granite-topped island in the kitchen and his suitcase bumped against his leg. He needed time alone to clear his head and sort out this mess, to get showered and changed, then get some sleep. Whatever was going on here could wait until the morning when, hopefully, he'd be thinking and acting more rationally again. "Thank you for all you've done for me tonight."

It took a moment, but finally she opened the door and headed back out into the hall. "I'll be back at seven tomorrow morning to take you to work."

After she left, Max went to the master bedroom to unpack. This wasn't like him. Not at all. But there was something about Ayanna that set him alight inside like a roman candle. Which was damned inconvenient. He didn't need this in his life right now. Didn't want it. He was more than happy living in his self-imposed, emotionless bubble. Things were easier that way.

Determined to put tonight and Ms. Franklin out of his mind, Max finished putting away his things then strode into the attached bathroom to turn on the walk-in shower. Steam filled the room while he stripped down then stepped beneath the shower head and let the hot water ease away the tension from his stiff muscles.

Regardless of this unwanted awareness where Ayanna was concerned, his best move was to ignore it. There were already far too many things that could go wrong here in

Seattle with the King's case.

His personal life didn't need to be added to the list.

CHAPTER FOUR

AN HOUR LATER, Ayanna slumped down on the cushy sofa in her apartment and toed off her pumps. Dealing with Max Granger had been an unexpected challenge in an already difficult day.

With a sigh, she took off her jacket and got out her laptop to pull up the spreadsheets she'd downloaded from her work computer earlier. It was going on two a.m. now and she should really try to sleep, but she had too much to do. Plus, she needed to start packing some of her stuff, since she needed to be out of her apartment by the end of the week so the workmen could get in. Not to mention the fact she was far too amped to sleep at this point from her earlier encounter with Max. She hoped maybe being productive would help lower her stress levels.

She started going over the lists of decorations needed for the ball and the menus and the musical selections, but time and again her mind kept circling back to Max Granger. For some reason, arguing with him had gotten her blood boiling, in more ways than one. Even now, if she closed her eyes, Ayanna could still remember the heat of him scorching through her clothes, could still smell the soap and cedar scent of his skin, could still hear the snarkiness in his tone during his comment in the changing room. And those icy gray-green eyes of his? They hadn't been frigid at all then. Nope. His gaze had been hot. Hot as the flames licking inside her now and…

Oh, boy.

She didn't *want* to want Dr. Max Granger that way. They'd just met. She didn't do love or romance or relationships anymore. Not after Will. She didn't believe in happily ever after. Having your fiancé run off with your best friend weeks before the wedding did that to a girl.

These days she was all about her career and fully intended to keep it that way, thanks so much. Never mind Max's growly, brooding alpha act called to her inner fixer. The only reason she was shadowing him was because that was her job. Dr. di Rossi expected her to keep the neurosurgeon reined in and that's exactly what she intended to do, whether Max liked it or not.

Taking a deep breath, she sat forward, determined to think about something else other than her infuriating new charge. The ball. That should be her focus. She'd throw the biggest and best holiday fundraising ball Seattle General had ever seen.

Fingers flying across her keyboard as she typed, Ayanna periodically checked her phone for updates and emails, and soon enough lost herself in her work. By the time she looked up again, it was almost five in the morning. Her muscles felt stiff from sitting in one spot too long and a glance out the window above her kitchen sink showed the first streaks of pink and purple near the horizon. So much for sleep. She stood and stretched, then froze in place at the sound of her phone buzzing on the coffee table. The number wasn't one she recognized, and she frowned down at the text message on her screen.

Not her family. Not her staff. Her pulse tripped.

Max.

She'd left a sheet of important numbers on the counter in the suite when they'd first arrived, hers being one of them, but she'd never expected him to use it. Her stomach dropped. Oh, God. What if the King had taken a turn for the worse? What if Max had once more rushed off, leaving her to scramble after him?

But as she read the message, her worry turned to surprise. Not an emergency at all, but an apology.

Thank you again for getting this suite. It's very nice and I appreciate it.

Stunned, Ayanna just blinked at her phone. Just when she'd put him squarely in the lump-of-coal-in-his-stocking category he went and did something nice. Not just nice—sweet. And that was…wow. The tension between her shoulder blades eased and her thumbs shook slightly as she typed in a response.

My pleasure. See you soon. A

After hitting "send" Ayanna sank back down on to the sofa and stared out the window for a long moment. She'd seen him be kind and solicitous to the nurses at the hospital, but that was the first time he'd done so with her and darn if that didn't make her see him in a better light. Maybe there was a chance they could make this work after all. Maybe they were both just trying to get through a difficult time as best they could. And maybe being around Max Granger wouldn't be quiet so tedious after all.

Early the next morning, Max ate his eggs and turkey sausage and drank his coffee, periodically peeking at his breakfast guest across the table from him over the top of his *New York Times*. Ayanna hadn't eaten a thing since she'd arrived promptly at seven, had just sat there working on her laptop and drinking coffee. Honestly, it was none of his business. He shouldn't say anything, especially after establishing their uneasy accord with his apology earlier, but he couldn't seem to stop himself.

"Are you feeling all right?' he asked, staring at his paper and not at her.

"Fine." She glanced up at him then continued typing. "Why?"

"No reason." He picked up his own buzzing phone to see another update from the ICU nurse on duty. The King was still stable and unconscious, but that wasn't uncommon after a bad concussion. The most important thing, his intracranial pressure, was holding at pre-accident levels, meaning no new clots had formed. Max clicked off his device and placed it face down on the table. "You aren't hungry?"

"Nah. I hardly ever eat in the morning." She leaned in closer to her screen and squinted at it before tapping a few more keys then smiling. That weird buzz flared inside him again. Things were finally smoothed over between them and he didn't need to ruffle them up again by drooling over the last person on earth he should be attracted to. Besides, Ayanna was too bright and bold and bubbly. He preferred quiet, calm, and routine these days. Bad enough they were sharing commutes, which meant seeing her each morning and evening. Restlessness niggled inside him again, but before it could take hold Ayanna's voice broke through the gathering shadows inside him like the rays of persistent sunshine burst through the clouds outside.

"Breakfast slows me down and makes me feel sluggish. I usually don't have time anyway." Ayanna glanced at his plate of eggs and meat. "You on a keto diet?"

"No." He swallowed another bite of turkey sausage. "Just like to get my protein. Helps my energy levels during long, busy days."

"Hmm." Sounding skeptical, she closed her laptop then nabbed a wedge of whole wheat toast from the plate he'd ordered, in case she wanted something. "Thanks again for your message this morning, by the way. I'm glad we're on better terms now."

He nodded, focusing on his scrambled eggs and not her. He still couldn't quite believe he'd sent that text, but in the moment it had seemed like the right thing to do. One of them had to give, and he could accept defeat. What he couldn't accept, however, were these appalling bad eggs. He wrinkled his nose.

"What's wrong?" Ayanna asked, giving him a wary look. "Don't tell me you're rescinding the apology now."

"What?" Max looked up and blinked at her, taking a second to connect the dots. "No. Nothing's wrong. Not about that, anyway. It's just these eggs aren't nearly as good as the ones I make."

Her expression turned dubious. "You cook?"

"I do." For some reason, people didn't expect him to know his way around a kitchen, but after his wife had died he'd had to fend for himself. Now Max considered himself a foodie. It was one of the few hobbies he had and he treasured his time in the kitchen, tinkering with new recipes. It helped relax him. "At first out of necessity and now because I enjoy it."

"Huh." She swallowed another bite of toast. "Well, your wife probably appreciates that."

He winced before he could stop himself. "My wife died two years ago."

"Oh." Ayanna flushed, setting the rest of her toast aside, uneaten. "I'm sorry. I had no idea."

"It's fine." Max shoved a whole sausage link in his mouth, chewing without tasting it. He expected the same hollow emptiness to fill him each time he thought of his life post-Laura, but for the first time in recent memory it didn't. He didn't stop to consider why, though, just swallowed his food with gulp of hot decaf tea, the scald on his throat a welcome distraction. "Anyway, eating out a lot isn't healthy, so I started buying a few cookbooks and trying my hand at things."

Ayanna tilted her head, her gaze narrowed. "And how'd that go?"

"At first? Not good." Max chuckled. "Right out of the gate I ruined an expensive set of pans because I burned everything I touched. Eventually, though, I got better. Even took some classes at Le Cordon Bleu in New York between cases. Now, I make a mean *coq au vin* and my scrambled eggs are the best in Manhattan."

"Huh. Maybe you can make me dinner some time." Ayanna's smile froze then faltered and she looked away fast, the silence between them turning awkward. To cover it, she refilled her coffee cup, for the third time by his estimation. He wasn't sure what she did with all that caffeine, but he avoided the stuff in order to hold his instruments steady.

While finishing the rest of his breakfast, Max studied her more closely as she frowned down into her mug. Dark smudges marred the delicate skin beneath her eyes today and there were new faint lines of stress at the corners of her lips. A pang of guilt stabbed his chest. He hoped their argument the night before hadn't been the cause of her lost sleep. She glanced up and caught him staring and he looked away.

She shrugged and sat back crossing her legs away from him. "Personally, I don't really cook at all, which is an affront to my mother who makes enormous meals whenever she can."

"You come from a big family?" he asked, glad to have a talking point again. Chatting with her was nice, normal. Ayanna was surprisingly easy to talk to—when she wasn't arguing with him, of course. "Are you married?"

"Yes and no," Ayanna said. "I have five younger siblings, two brothers and three sisters, and we all love to eat. And I was engaged once, but things didn't work out."

He wanted to ask more, but her firm tone effectively shut the door on that topic. Just as well, since he had no business getting more involved with her life. He stood to set the room service tray in the kitchen. Truth was, he'd missed this kind of morning routine. Missed making small talk over the table. Missed connecting with another person, no matter how trivial the topic.

When he'd met Laura, she'd pulled him out of the isolation of his youth. Being with her had taught him that love and affection were normal and nice and needed. Now that she was gone, deep down part of him feared falling back into that same trap again, feared squeezing back inside the cold, unfeeling shell his parents had raised him in. After living with his wife, those tight confines of emotionlessness didn't fit as comfortably anymore and that knowledge both worried and terrified him.

"If cooking is your thing, I can call today and have groceries delivered so you can use the kitchen here in the suite. All of the appliances work," Ayanna said, following him into the kitchen to rinse out her cup in the sink. "Just give me a list of what you need and I'll make sure it's all here this evening."

At first, he was going to tell her not to bother, since he planned to talk to the head of neurosurgery today about consulting on some additional cases to keep busy—there was also no telling if or when the King's condition might change—but then he reconsidered. Cooking was his go-to stress reliever. No matter what, he still had to eat. Making food helped clear his head and he could use a breather right now. "Okay. That would be nice. Thank you for offering."

"You're welcome." Ayanna checked her watch. "We should get going. Traffic's a bear in the mornings and I've got a pile of work to get done today."

"Sure." Max tugged on his jacket while Ayanna gathered her computer and bag. Maybe this whole carpool thing would work out better than he'd imagined. "And if I cook, maybe I can get you to eat."

Ayanna glanced up at him, flashing that sunny smile of hers again, and his day got a tad brighter. "Maybe. We'll see. You've got a few weeks to try anyway."

CHAPTER FIVE

LATER THAT MORNING, after checking in on
the King's condition—stable but still unconscious—and reporting his finding to Dr. di
Rossi, Max headed between buildings at Seattle General. He liked to stay busy and since
the King's prognosis was still uncertain, Max
had cleared his calendar until after the first
of the new year and planned to hunker down
here in Seattle until then.

Luckily, the chief of neurosurgery was
running short on staff with the holidays.
Many of the doctors took time off to be with
their families, so the department was eager
to have Max's help. In fact, he'd barely finished filling out his paperwork downstairs in
HR and got hold of his staff pass when a call
came in from the ER that they had a new patient who needed a neuro consult.

He headed through the maze of brightly
lit halls, his attention split between the busy

Seattle streets below and the facilities around him. Max was still learning his way around the place, but so far he'd been impressed. They had state-of-the-art equipment and were participating in several prominent clinical trials. Dr. di Rossi ran a tight ship in the ER as well, erasing any doubts Max might have had that the King had only chosen this facility for his surgery because of his son.

And, much as he hated to admit it, part of his mind was still focused on Ayanna. He wasn't sure why exactly, but she intrigued him far more than anyone else had in a long time. Delicious smells wafted from the cafeteria and he pulled out his phone to add some baking ingredients to the list of items he'd asked Ayanna to order for him earlier.

Truthfully, he looked forward to cooking like some men looked forward to the NFL playoffs. He hadn't been kidding about getting her to eat better while he was here either. In fact, he took it as a personal challenge to get her have breakfast each day when she came to pick him up. He'd already asked her to get the necessary ingredients to make his signature roasted vegetable frittata for her tomorrow: zucchini, bell peppers, onions, garlic, cream, eggs and Parmesan cheese. Seeing the look of ecstasy on her face when she tasted the first bite would be reward enough for getting up extra early to prepare it.

But as he continued on through the busy corridors toward the ER, Max's visions of Ayanna groaning with delight over his food suddenly morphed into something else entirely, his mind filling with images of the two of them entwined in his sheets, her soft moans parting those delectable lips as she called out his name when she came apart in his arms...

What the...?

Max stopped short, narrowly avoiding crashing into several other people walking towards him.

Thinking about sex with Ayanna made no sense. They barely knew each other. They had been thrown together because of the King's case, that was all. Besides, he wasn't looking for intimacy. Things were complicated enough in his life without opening himself up to that too. And, yes, he was a normal, straight guy. He dealt with his libido by sleeping only with women who understood the rules—no fuss, no muss, and certainly no emotions or strings attached. From the brief time he'd spent with Ayanna, she didn't seem like the type of woman who had affairs or flings.

The whole idea was insane. Impossible. Yet far more compelling than he cared to admit.

He stepped around the group of visitors blocking his path, then continued toward the ER. Keeping things strictly professional with Ayanna during his stay in Seattle was priority one. After losing Laura, Max never wanted to open himself up to being emotionally vulnerable again. He was perfectly happy in his isolated, rational bubble. There was safety in being alone. He'd much rather deal with that than have his heart shredded. No. His parents had had it right. Emotions only caused trouble. Rubbing his hand over his tight chest, he jogged down the remaining stairs, resignation dogging his heels as he entered the emergency department.

"What's the rundown?" Max asked Dr. Cho, the resident who'd called him in for a consult, while he clicked through the case file at a computer terminal in the hall.

"Seventeen-year-old male with positive loss of consciousness after being slammed into the boards while playing hockey," Dr. Cho said, her dark spiky hair gleaming midnight blue beneath the lights.

"How long was he out?"

"About three minutes, according to witnesses."

Max scrolled through the patient's vitals, which all looked good, then headed into the room where the kid was now awake and talking to his parents, who sat anxiously by his bedside. He shook their hands, then turned to the patient. "Hi. there. I'm Dr. Granger. Can you tell me your name?"

"Josh Whitaker." The kid frowned. "Why am I here?"

"Because you hit your head." Max took a penlight from the pocket of his scrub shirt and checked the teen's pupils—both equal and reactive to light—then gently examined the patient's skull for signs of a possible fracture. There was a nasty cut over his left eyebrow, but otherwise the boy seemed uninjured. "Can you tell me if anything hurts where I'm pushing?"

"Nothing hurts." Josh winced as his arm hit the bed rail. "My hand's numb, though, and I feel dizzy."

"Okay." Max finished examining Josh then stepped back to record his findings in the electronic file. Head injuries were always concerning in someone this young. Unfortunately, they weren't all that uncommon, especially in contact sports like hockey, football and soccer. As Max typed, he continued to ask questions over his shoulder. "Josh, do you remember anything about what happened?"

"Uh…" Josh scowled then ran his fingers through his messy blond hair. "The last thing I remember was… I don't know. No, I don't think I remember anything at all."

"Okay." Max glanced at the parents. "Has he had previous concussions?"

"Yes," Josh's mother said, her tone concerned. "About two years ago, when he was playing lacrosse. Will my son be okay, Doctor?"

Max wanted to say yes but the fact that Josh had had multiple head injuries prior to today wasn't ideal. Still, he tried to be as encouraging as possible. "We'll do everything we can, Mrs. Whitaker."

She closed her eyes as her husband put his arm around her. "I've seen my son get hit a lot, but I didn't think it was that bad this time. But he just lay there on the ice, not moving, and they called the coach and then 911…" Her shoulders shook with sobs and Mr. Whitaker handed her a tissue.

"As I said, we'll do everything we can for Josh." Max did his best to reassure her. The teen was young and strong and he should be fine.

Laura should've been fine too.

Max coughed and shoved aside his past failings and guilt to focus on the case at hand. "We'll get an MRI to have an idea of what's happening in his brain. If that's clear, then I'd say your son likely has a concussion. Let's wait on the results then go from there, all right?"

"Yes." Ms. Whitaker reached over and took Max's hand. "Thank you, Doctor."

"My pleasure." Helping others was why Max had gone into neurosurgery in the first place and the fact these poor people were spending their day in a hospital instead of out preparing for the holidays like everyone else only made him more determined to do what he could. Just because he didn't do Christmas anymore, it didn't mean the Whitakers didn't deserve to have their son home and healthy for the season. "Let me call Radiology and get things rolling."

At the nurses' station Max put in a stat call for an MRI then waited until the technicians wheeled Josh away. While he waited for results, Max went upstairs to ICU to check in on King Roberto again. Still no change. Disappointing but not too discouraging, since short-term comas weren't uncommon after a craniotomy.

* * *

Twenty minutes later Max got a text that Josh's MRI was complete, and the results were ready for him to view. He returned to the ER and brought up the images on the computer in Josh's trauma bay.

Josh seemed to be in a bit better spirits at least, which was a good sign.

"Do I have a brain, Doc?" he joked.

Max snorted. "Yep. It's still in there."

He scrolled through the images then turned to the anxious parents. "The good news is there's no sign of any internal bleeding in the brain or clotting and no skull fractures either. But given his pain and dizziness and the fact he hit a wall hard with his head, your son most likely has a concussion." Max shut off the computer and crossed his arms, narrowing his gaze on the patient. "Which means no hockey for a while, son."

Josh gave a disappointed sigh.

"I know it's hard, but you need time to heal," Max continued. "A few weeks at least, until your brain recovers, and you can have a checkup with your regular doctor. Then when you do go back on the ice, make sure you have on your safety gear. Understood?"

"Understood, Doc," Josh said, then turned to his dad. "Did we at least win?"

His dad laughed. "Yep, son. Three to nothing."

Max exited the trauma bay to finish Josh's discharge paperwork, relief lifting a bit of burden off his shoulders. Cases like King Roberto's, where progress was slow, made for long days and worrisome nights. Having a case like Josh's with a swifter positive outcome helped ease the strain. After he completed his documentation, he turned the case back over to Dr. Cho then decided to take a walk.

Being cooped up in one place too long made him stir crazy, another unexpected side effect of his hectic work schedule. He grabbed a lab coat off one of the racks of spare scrubs against the wall, then pushed outside through a side exit door. For a Sunday in late November, the temperatures in Seattle were surprisingly moderate, though the sky was a typical overcast gray. Weak sunlight filtered through the clouds above and people rushed down the busy sidewalks, even on a weekend. Heading down Terry Street toward Madison, his stomach growled, and he checked his watch. Yep, it was lunchtime. Maybe he'd sample some local cuisine while he was out and about.

Passing by a sign for Zipcar, his thought

returned to Ayanna. Zippy certainly described her. She seemed to go twenty-four seven, always working, always moving. Not that he had any room to talk. He was Type A through and through as well. Neurosurgery wasn't for slackers, as his parents used to remind him all the time. Too bad, since he could've used a little more downtime with them to just be a kid, just enjoy his childhood and feel like he was loved.

An image of Josh and his family flashed through his head. They'd been so easy and affectionate with each other, so different from how *he* had grown up. His thoughts circled around to what Ayanna had told him earlier about her own family. Five siblings. Wow. He couldn't imagine what that must've been like, growing up with all that noise and togetherness and love. He'd grown up with loneliness and nannies. Yet even from a distance his parents had pushed him to succeed, to do better, to be better. They'd cared little for his heart. For them, it was all about his mind. Looking back, he supposed they'd meant to encourage him, but he didn't really know for sure. All he knew was that they'd remained remote and emotionally distant from him when what he'd really craved was closeness and compassion. Eventually, when his repeated efforts to engage them emotionally had failed, he'd learned to switch off his emotions and interact with them on a purely cerebral level in order to get any attention at all.

Laura had used to joke with him about being able to "flip the switch", as she'd called it, when he was working, but honestly, it hadn't been until he'd married her that he'd finally escaped that buttoned-up, locked-down emotional state and learned to feel again.

Now, though, since her death, he'd retreated back into isolation again.

An image of Ayanna this morning popped into his head, with her perfectly pressed crimson pantsuit, her sunny smile and her bright eyes. Maybe that's why he couldn't seem to stop thinking about her. She reminded him of the connection and vitality he'd lost. First with his parents and then again two years ago when Laura had died.

A door opened nearby and warm air gusted around him, scented with fresh baked bread and cinnamon. Memories of making cinnamon rolls with Laura on Christmas morning flooded his mind and for a moment it felt like a hug from the beyond. Max blinked hard to stem the yearning inside him. He was happy alone. He didn't need anyone else in his life.

He didn't *want* to need anyone else again.

Through the glass windows of the bakery, golden lights beckoned him inside. A handwritten chalk menu by the door listed all sorts of delicious-sounding sandwiches and Max went inside to grab lunch. As he waited to order, Christmas carols drifted from the stereo system, though he found them less annoying today, for some reason.

While he stood in line, he pulled out his phone to check for updates and instead found a text from Ayanna. The sight of her name on his screen sent a thrill of adrenaline through his system, which was weird. According to the message, she was running late, buried under work, and she might not be ready to go at five, as originally scheduled. She also said she'd placed his delivery order and it would be waiting at the suite once they arrived.

All righty, then. He knew from personal experience how easy it was to let things like meals slide when you got busy. But as a physician he also knew the importance of good nutrition for keeping a healthy immune system. With winter on their doorstep and her being his ride to and from the hospital, he needed her to stay healthy. Besides, the idea of Ayanna neglecting herself bothered Max more than he cared to admit. She'd already skipped breakfast. He refused to let her skip lunch too, as he suspected she would from her text.

"Welcome to the Thunderbird Café," a woman behind the counter greeted him. "May I take your order?"

Max stepped up and ordered two Turkey Havarti sandwiches, and kale chips to go. Honestly, he had no idea what Ayanna liked, other than coffee, but figured it was worth a shot. After paying and grabbing their food, he headed back to Seattle General.

Ayanna ended her call and laid her head atop her arms on the desk in her office. As if she didn't have enough to deal with at present, that had been the Polar Club stating that due to a staff error the ballroom had been double-booked for December twelfth, the night of the hospital's ball. After a battle with the functions manager at the hotel the ballroom was theirs, but still. A girl only had so much time and patience to go around and Ayanna had not planned to spend all hers on that.

With a sigh, she straightened and smoothed a hand down the front of her new wool suit, taking a deep breath before staring at the stack of files on her desk once more. Her hands shook slightly from low blood sugar, so she took another swig of her energy drink before diving back into planning the ball décor again. She'd barely begun on the table centerpieces when a knock on the door interrupted her.

"Yes?" she called, without looking up, doing her best to keep the irritation from her tone and failing. The door opened and Ayanna expected to see one of her staff walk in with yet another problem for her to solve, but instead she was greeted by the sight of Max Granger holding food and two bottles of water. How the man managed to make a plain white lab coat and scrubs look so sexy was a mystery.

"Good afternoon," he said, smiling then closing the door behind him before taking a seat in one of the chairs in front of her desk. She'd been around enough powerful men in her line of work to know they tended to act like they owned the place, no matter where they went. Will had been that way too, working in finance. With her ex it had rubbed her up the wrong way on occasion, but then again Will had never brought her lunch on a hectic day either. Of course, he'd been fine with her doing it for him, though. Even though he'd complained about her busy schedule, he'd never once complained about her doing all sorts of little things to make his life easier. Nope. In fact, he'd taken her generosity for granted.

Max, though, had been nothing but sweet to her since they'd made peace. He placed one of the bags and a bottle of water on the desk beside her energy drink and grinned, the color of his eyes reminding her of the waters of Puget Sound during a storm. "It's past lunchtime and I thought you might be hungry now. Can't having you missing another meal."

Ayanna blinked at him for a moment, then spotted the logo from her favorite café. Growing up, she'd always been the caretaker, the one looking out for everyone else. It felt odd to receive that sort of attention from someone else. Odd and a bit scary, to be honest. Because having someone take care of her for a change scratched an invisible itch she hadn't even known she had until now. Her stomach growled and she peeked inside the bag. "Um, thank you."

"My pleasure," he said, winking as he opened his own bag and pulled out a paper-wrapped sandwich and a bag of kale chips. "I did warn you."

"Warn me?" Her brows drew together as she discovered the same turkey sandwich and a bag of chips inside her own sack. Ayanna quickly unwrapped it and took a bite, chewing and swallowing before she asked, "About what?"

"About you eating properly." He gulped down a large swig of water. "At breakfast this morning. Studies show keeping your blood sugar levels steady through the day by eating regularly helps increase productivity. Coffee and energy drinks only solve the problem temporarily. Eventually you crash, harder than you would have with food. It's a vicious cycle."

She snorted around a mouthful of salty kale chips. "Thanks, Mr. Food Police."

"Anytime." Max grinned and her insides gave a tiny, unwanted flutter. She stared down at her food, anywhere but at him, as she ate. Whatever this weird attraction was, she needed to get over it quickly. She had far too much to deal with as it was. She didn't need her neglected girly parts chiming in.

Max ate another large bite of his sandwich then pointed to the files on her overflowing desktop. "What are you working on?"

"One issue after another, unfortunately." She started to tell him all about her problems with the ball, but then stopped. Sharing her burdens wasn't exactly a skill she'd honed. It was hard enough delegating things to her staff, let alone telling someone about issues with her new job. Even if he did seem to be a good listener, the last thing he probably wanted to hear about were flowers and hors d'oeuvres. So she dodged his with a question of her own. "How is the King?"

"Stable. Tell me more about this ball. What's your menu?" Max asked, refusing to be deterred. He was stubborn too, apparently. A good trait in a surgeon. Maybe not so much in a lunch companion. "I'm a foodie, remember? Maybe I can help."

"You want to help me with the planning?" She gave him a dubious stare, but it made sense. And much as she hated to admit it, she was used to designing global PR campaigns, not picking out entrées and desserts. Maybe she should take him up on his offer. He was sitting here in her office anyway, so what could it hurt? She set her sandwich down and flipped open a folder again before turning it to face him. "Well, since you insist, I'm having fits trying to get the hospital's big fundraising ball planned in half the time it normally takes."

"Hmm." He finished off his kale chips

then stuffed the debris back inside his sack before reaching for the centerpiece photos. "Sounds stressful. What have you done so far?"

"The only thing that's locked down at this point is the venue. It's being held in the ballroom of the hotel where you're staying. I just got off the phone with the Polar Club, actually. Apparently, they double booked our ballroom for the same evening, but my predecessor made our reservation first, so the was crisis averted, thankfully. Now, I'm going over décor options for the ballroom then I need to pick menus for the night and book musicians and—"

Her cellphone rang, cutting her off. Par for the course when it came to interruptions today. Ayanna held up a finger for Max to wait, then answered without checking the caller ID. "Ayanna Franklin."

"Hi, honey. How are you?" her mother said, the sound of cooking in the background as usual. Ayanna loved her mom, loved her whole family, but this was another time suck she didn't need, especially since she was pretty sure her mother was calling about Thanksgiving, and also about Ayanna staying there while her apartment was being worked on. More things to add to her to-do list.

"I'm fine, Mom. Busy." Ayanna swiveled away from Max for a modicum of privacy and faced the bookshelves covering one wall of her office. "What did you need?"

"I wanted to let you know your room's ready to go," her mother said. "We can talk about Thanksgiving after you get moved in again."

"I'm not moving back in, Mom." Ayanna glanced back over her shoulder at Max, who'd grown suspiciously quiet, only to find him riffling through more event files on her desk. Shocked, she swung her chair around to smack his hand away. "At most I'll only be staying there a few weeks until the electrical work is done at my place."

Max glanced up at her and quirked an inquisitive brow, which she ignored. She gave him a "don't touch" look then turned back to face her bookcases again.

"And where else are you going to stay, huh?" her mom said. "James is out of town. So are Clarissa and Tonya. I don't know about LaTasha or Brandon, but you know how they are. So that counts out your siblings, which leaves your old room, honey."

"I'm thinking maybe I'll get a hotel room," Ayanna said, cradling the phone between her shoulder and wincing at her mother's outraged gasp. "It's not that I don't want to see you guys, it's just that I've got a lot of work to do over the next couple of weeks and I really need a distraction-free space to do it in."

"Distraction, huh?" Her mother gave an imperious sniff. "Is that how you see us now?"

Ayanna closed her eyes and rubbed the bridge of her nose. No one played the guilt card better than a mother. "No, Mom. It's not that at all, it's just—"

"Just what?" her mom asked, her tone skeptical. "If you think you're going to worm your way out of Thanksgiving dinner with us, you've got another think coming. I've already bought the turkey and all the stuff for side dishes. I will not waste all this food because you think your fancy job is more important than being home for the holidays—you got me, young lady?"

And just like that, Ayanna was back to being ten years old again, getting a dressing down from Momma because she'd let her brothers make a mess in the garage when she was supposed to be watching them. Shame flared hot in her chest before she tamped it down. "No. I'll be there for Thanksgiving."

She actually *had* been planning on cancelling, not because she didn't want to see her family but because of her crazy schedule. But if showing up got her off the hook with her mom about staying with them during her apartment work, then so be it. Even if she didn't have another place to stay. Yet.

"Well, I suppose that's something, at least," her mother said, banging a pan on the stove. "Your father just bought a thirty-pound turkey. Do you know how many people a thirty-pound turkey feeds?"

"No."

"Twenty-five people, that's how many," her mother continued over Ayanna's answer. "Plus, I've got potatoes and stuffing and rolls and pie. Three pumpkin pies. Darn right you'll be here on the holiday because who else is going to help me get all this ready?"

Ayanna was tempted to give a smartass answer then reconsidered. Sassing her mother when she was pissed was taking her life into her hands. Thankfully, she was saved by the call-waiting beep. "Hang on, Mom."

She abruptly switched lines, cutting off her mother's continued speech about starving people in Africa, and said in her best PR director tone, "Ayanna Franklin, how may I help you?"

All the while Max sat across from her, watching her with an inscrutable expression. Her cheeks heated and she did her best to concentrate on the person talking on the other end of the line. She didn't like appearing anything less that poised in front of other people, especially Max.

"Yes, Ms. Franklin. This is Gerry Miller with the Thunderbird Orchestra returning your call," the guy on the other end of the line said.

Right. The musicians. She sifted through the paperwork in front of her, searching for their fact sheet as her mother's call buzzed on the other line. Her breath hitched and she bumped her water bottle, nearly knocking it over, but Max caught it. Dammit. Where was that paper?

Buzz. Buzz. Buzz.

"Sorry," she said, forcing the words past her tight vocal cords. "Can you hang on a moment, Mr. Miller? I'm just finishing up with another call."

She put the musician back on hold then picked up with her mother again. "Sorry, Mom. I have to go. I'll call you later, okay?"

"Okay," her mother huffed out. "And let me know what time you'll be here on Thanksgiving too."

"I will."

As soon as I figure that out myself.

Ayanna stared over at Max as she ended the call, then picked up again with the musician. By the time she'd gotten the band sorted out, Max had thrown away his trash. Ayanna had expected him to leave once he'd eaten, but instead he flopped back down in his chair and steepled his fingers. "What's happening at your apartment?"

"They're doing some electrical work. I need to stay elsewhere until it's done." She took another drink of water to dislodge the lingering lump of stress from her throat. "Why?"

"You don't want to stay with your parents?"

"No, I'd rather not sleep in my tiny twin bed again. Besides, I need some privacy while I sort out this mess with the ball and that's in short supply at my parents' house most of the time."

"Hmm." Max tapped his fingers against his lips, seemingly deep in thought. "You told your mother you were getting a hotel room."

"Yeah?" Ayanna sat back, taking another bite of her sandwich. "So?"

"So you told me the other night that mine was the only room left in town."

Ayanna swallowed. Dammit. Why did he have to be so observant? She could've told

Will the same information fifty times and he still wouldn't have remembered. But Max Granger had a memory like a steel trap. Just one more annoying trait on her growing list of things about him that got under her skin, and it bothered her more than she cared to admit. Straightening slightly, she finished the last bite of her sandwich before answering. "And?"

"And you just lied to your mother."

Out of patience, she balled up her empty wrapper and tossed it in the bin with more force than necessary. She'd save the kale chips for a snack later. "Why is my private life any of your business? And like you never lied to your parents. Everyone has at one time or another."

"Not mine." A shadow passed over his face, sadness maybe or resignation. Either way, his broad shoulders slumped a bit. "I wasn't close enough to lie to them."

She took that in, not sure what to say. That sounded really odd. And horrible. How could someone not be close to their own parents? Her family drove her nuts sometimes, but they were always there whenever she needed them. Ayanna didn't like the fact she'd lied to her mom, but she liked even less that Dr.

Granger now looked like someone had kicked his puppy. "I'm sorry."

Max exhaled, watching her a moment as if coming to some decision. "You should stay with me."

"Excuse me?" She couldn't have heard that right.

"The suite has two bedrooms. Seems a waste of space to leave one empty when you're in need of lodgings." He sat forward. "Plus, since we're riding together to and from work, it makes sense for you to stay there. We don't have to interact any more than we already are. You'll have separate sleeping quarters and a separate bathroom. You can work on your ball preparations and I can continue to plan for the King's surgery on the fifteenth." Max stood and pointed at the files on her desk. "Plus, you'll be onsite to meet with the musicians and chefs for the party."

"Well, I…" Ayanna wanted to argue with him about it, but damn if he wasn't right. It did make sense, no matter how much she might wish it didn't.

"Think about it," he said, walking to the door. "Let me know tonight. See you in the Seneca Lot when you're ready. Just text me. Oh." He turned to look at her over his shoulder. "And thanks for ordering the groceries."

After he'd gone, she sat staring at the closed door, wondering what the hell had just happened.

CHAPTER SIX

MAX FINISHED PUTTING away the groceries Ayanna had ordered, still a bit shocked at himself for suggesting that they share the suite. Too late now, though, since she'd accepted his offer and was currently on her way back here with her bags. He checked the cupboards in the kitchen then pulled out several frying pans and a couple of mixing bowls and set them on the granite island beside the package of skinless chicken breasts and fresh veggies he planned to cook for dinner.

As he cleaned and chopped and prepared the food to stir fry it, he felt some of the stress from his day leave his body. After his lunch with Ayanna in her office, he'd gone back to his interim office down the hall in Neurology and gotten to work on plans to have a 3D model of the King's brain tumor made from the MRIs and CT scans his patient had had done recently by a company affiliated with

Seattle General. It was cutting-edge technology and would help Max better prepare for the surgery ahead.

Once he'd heated the sesame oil in the pan, he dumped the veggies in and stirred them around until their heavenly scents filled the air. He also started a pot of water to make the rice. Before he knew it, the suite smelled fantastic and there was a knock on the door.

An unexpected jolt of eagerness jangled through him as he hurried to let Ayanna into the suite. Normally, he prized his alone time above all else, but tonight he looked forward to getting to know her better.

"Here, let me help you with those." He took the case from over her shoulder as she trundled into the suite with what looked like enough luggage for three people. Ayanna headed toward the second bedroom with a large wheeled suitcase in one hand and two smaller ones in the other, stacked one atop the other. "You're only planning on staying a few weeks, right?"

"Less, if I can help it," Ayanna said. How she maneuvered all this stuff with her small frame and in those ridiculous heels, he had no idea. "As soon as another room opens up here, I'm taking it. Why?"

"You seem to have enough clothes for the next year." Max chuckled.

"I like to have options in what I wear." He followed her down the hall and watched as she set her bags near the end of the queen-sized bed. "And in my job, appearance is important."

"Sure." He nodded, still not completely convinced but smart enough not to argue with a woman about clothing. "Right. Well, I'll let you settle in while I check on dinner."

"What are you making? It smells amazing."

"Chicken stir fry. Hope you're hungry."

"I am." Ayanna turned to unzip the closest suitcase to her. "And thank you for letting me stay here."

"No problem." He backed away slowly, reluctant to leave. It wasn't like they were anything more than acquaintances, yet he felt drawn to her far more than he had to anyone in a long time. Warmth spread upward from beneath the collar of the gray sweatshirt he'd changed into after work. He smoothed the palm of his hand down the thigh of his jeans then reached for the door handle. "See you in a bit."

"Yep." She grinned at him over her shoulder as she unpacked. "See you."

Want fizzed alongside the adrenaline in his system now.

This was bad. Very, very bad. He didn't *want* to want Ayanna that way. Didn't care to get close to anyone that way again. And yet he'd invited her to stay here, with him, in the same suite.

God, I'm an idiot.

As he finished cooking then dished up dinner onto serving plates, Max searched in vain for a way to make this work that wouldn't involve his libido getting any more involved where Ayanna was concerned. His analytical brain said they'd eat meals together, ride to and from the hospital. Maybe pass in the hall sometimes. That was all. He could do this.

But his heart pinched with the loneliness he'd kept buried for so long and that's what had him worried. Logically he could keep Ayanna in a tidy little box. But emotionally she awakened things in him without even trying—yearning, need, desire—things he'd thought he'd safely buried with Laura. All of them came surging back whenever Ayanna was around and that scared him more than any life-threatening surgery ever had.

Ayanna unpacked then changed into jeans and an oversized black Seahawks sweatshirt.

Staying here was ideal in a lot of ways, but less so in others. Namely the fact that she was sharing space with Max, the one man who'd made her sit up and take notice when she'd been able to avoid romance altogether since Will.

She'd done everything she could to stop her unwanted attraction to him in its tracks, but so far nothing had worked. So she planned to be kind and courteous and stay in her own lane while she was here. Not get any friendlier than necessary. Given how busy they both were, it shouldn't be a problem.

Except when she walked out of her room and down the hall and caught sight of Max in the kitchen, her heart gave a little flip. Man, oh, man. He had his back to her as he cooked, his lithe, muscled build and graceful movements captivating her. He was just her type, if she'd been looking. Tall, dark and gorgeous, with that whole brooding thing going on.

Down, girl. Down. Remember what happened with Will. He was your type too. Until he wasn't anymore.

Will's betrayal had left Ayanna questioning everything, most of all her instincts. She'd been wrong once. What's to say she wouldn't be wrong again? And no matter how Max's inner demons might pull on her heartstrings and make her want to take care of him, she couldn't do that again. Will's betrayal had almost broken her. Going through that again might just end her, once and for all.

Forcing a cheerful smile she didn't quite feel, Ayanna squared her shoulders and headed into the living room in her stockinged feet. Fake it till you make it, wasn't that the motto? She cleared her throat to alert Max to her presence then rubbed her hands on the thighs of her faded jeans. "Anything I can help with?"

"You can set the table, if you want," he said, pointing with his spatula to a stack of plates and silverware on the island. "Drinks too. I'm good with water, but there's also soda in the mini-bar. Or liquor, if you prefer."

"Water's good for me too," Ayanna said, grabbing the plates, grateful she'd tied her hair back into a low ponytail to keep it out of the way. At work, she dressed to kill, but at home she liked to be comfy and cozy. Wanting to keep the relaxed vibe going, she asked, "How was the rest of your afternoon?"

"Good." Max dished up their food then set the bowls on the table while Ayanna grabbed the bottles of water from the fridge. "Consulted on a couple of new patients, checked on the King again. Designed a model of his tumor for pre-surgery prep."

"A model?" Ayanna asked, as they sat down to eat. She dished herself up a large portion of rice and stir fry then dug into the spicy, savory sweetness with appreciation. "This is… Wow. You are a fabulous cook, Dr. Granger."

"Thanks, Ms. Franklin." He grinned and her toes curled. One of his front teeth was slightly crooked, overlapping the one next to it a bit. She'd never noticed that before. Instead of detracting from his handsomeness, the small imperfection only made him more gorgeous.

To distract herself, she frowned down at her food and continued their conversation. "Tell me more about this model thing. Sounds fascinating."

He went on about brain tumors and axial models and 3D printing while she did her best to take in all the details. Some of the terms were familiar from her mom's nursing work, but some of it went right over her head. Still, it was good to have someone else do the talking instead of her carrying the conversation load for a change. At first, getting Will to talk about his days had been like pulling teeth. Then later he'd only wanted to talk about himself. She squeezed her fork harder than necessary and glanced up at Max. He was looking at her expectantly and it took her a moment to realize he'd asked her something. Crap. She gulped some water to hide her embarrassment. "I'm sorry?"

"I asked how your afternoon went," he said around a mouthful of chicken and veggies. "Get any more done on the décor?"

"Some." She told him her plans for the lighting and the table runners, surprised and delighted he'd asked. "I'm still deciding on the centerpieces, though. There's a florist here in town who does beautiful work, but I'm not sure we have enough time to use them. When I was preparing for my wedding reception, they were booking four months ahead."

When she'd realized what she'd let slip, Ayanna winced. Damn. She'd not meant to bring up her past or Will again but, knowing Max, now that it was out he wouldn't let it drop. Sure enough, when she glanced over at him, he was watching her with that inscrutable look again.

"What?" she asked, trying to dissemble.

"Nothing." He stabbed more chicken with his fork, avoiding her gaze. "You'd mentioned you were engaged once before, but you're not married now."

"No. I'm not."

He paused in mid-bite, his gray gaze locked with hers. "I'm sorry."

"It's fine." She waved it off with her fork, shoveling in more food to push down the lingering hurt inside her that always resurfaced when the wedding was mentioned. Since she'd been a little girl, Ayanna had dreamed of her wedding day, how special it would be, how magical. Will had taken all of that away from her.

Bastard.

Max blinked at her for a moment then stared down at his food again. "Doesn't sound fine. I understand if you don't want to talk about it, though. Some painful things are best left in the past."

Ayanna should have stopped talking then. Should've eaten her dinner and been done with it, but for some reason she found herself telling Max all about it instead. "My fiancé's name was Will. Will Barnett. We'd known each other since high school and dated in college. He was in finance. Everyone thought we were the perfect couple. He proposed to me on New Year's Eve at the top of the freaking Space Needle." She drank more water to combat the bile burning in her throat and gave Max a rueful smile. "He was always Mr. Popular. Always knew the right thing to say. That's probably how he kept the affair hidden so long."

"Oh." Max scowled across the table at her. "That's awful."

"Yeah. It was bad. He ran off with my best friend, Rinna, a month before the wedding. Then blamed me for it. Said I wasn't supporting him enough. Said I put my career before everything. Said I was so busy taking care of other people that I never stopped to take care of him and our relationship. Never mind the fact that I bent over backward to always be there for him, to always lend a supporting ear, always doing things for him." She snorted, her laugh decidedly unpleasant. "Anyway. He's gone. They moved to LA two months ago, so…yeah." She cringed at Max's dark expression. "Sorry. Didn't mean to unload like that."

"Not at all." He finished his plate of food then stood to clear their dishes. "Thank you for sharing that with me."

"That's who I am," Ayanna said, getting up to help him clear the table, trying to mask her pain with a joke. "I'm a giver. Just ask Will. Or my family."

"Pardon my French, but he sounds like an ass," Max said, taking the plates from her to put in the sink. "You're well rid of him." He filled one half of the stainless-steel sink with soapy water then began to scrub. "And speaking of your family, did you tell your mother where you're staying?"

"I did." She grabbed a towel. "Not about us being here together or anything." She picked up a clean plate to dry, desperate to change the subject. "What about your family?"

Oh, crap. Why'd I ask that? With his wife and all and...

He set another clean plate in the drainer, the corners of his mouth tightening. "I don't have any family to speak of anymore. My wife passed away two years ago, and my parents died when I was eighteen."

Ayanna nodded, feeling terrible but not sure what to say. Her family were constantly in each other's business. She couldn't imagine a life where that wasn't the case. She shouldn't ask but couldn't seem to stop herself. He seemed so lonely and forlorn, standing there all alone, and her fixer genes kicked into overdrive. "What are you doing for Thanksgiving?"

"Working. Same as any other day." He

shrugged, not looking up from the sink. "Why?"

"My mother has got plenty of food and she loves having guests to fawn over." Ayanna dried the last dish then set her towel aside to put the clean plates away. "You're welcome to come with me to my parents' house, if you're not busy."

Maybe having him around would divert attention away from her and avoid the dreaded questions about her love life. His being there wouldn't hurt anything, would it? Of course, he'd have to say yes first.

"I don't know." Max drained the sink then hung the dishcloth over the center divider to dry. "I don't really do holidays anymore, like I said."

"Well, the invitation is open, if you change your mind." They finished up in the kitchen then went out into the living room. Ayanna shuffled her feet, the cold hardwood chilling her toes even through her socks. "Well, uh, I should go work on the plans for the ball some more, I guess. Thanks again for dinner."

"You're welcome," Max said, as she backed away toward the hall. "And thanks for the invitation. I'll think about it. Don't work too hard."

"Same to you." She watched him sit back

down on the sofa and open his laptop. She hadn't even been there one night yet and already this all felt natural, normal. And if that wasn't a sign to keep to herself even more, she didn't know what was. She had no business getting all comfortable and homey with Max Granger. Not now, not ever. "Goodnight."

"'Night." He smiled over at her. And darn if that little flutter in her gut didn't start all over again.

CHAPTER SEVEN

"Okay. Any questions before we walk in there?" Ayanna asked on Thursday morning as they pulled up to the curb outside her parents' blue and white craftsman-style home in the Seattle suburb of Redmond. Outside, the air was misty from the recent rain and clumps of snow from the last storm still dotted the ground. Typical Washington state weather for late November. At least the temperature wasn't bad at fifty-five. Several other cars already clogged the driveway and lined the curb out front, meaning the rest of her siblings had already arrived.

She parked then cut the engine, taking a few slow breaths to calm the rise in her pulse. She loved her family, but they could be...*a lot*. Especially for someone from the outside like Max. Honestly, Ayanna had second-guessed her decision to invite him along today at least a billion times since their dinner together on Sunday night, but in the end she just couldn't stand the thought of him sitting alone in the suite during the holiday, since they were both off work today. Besides, he'd been nice enough to cook for her and let her stay in his suite. The least she could do was repay the favor.

A glance at the front bay windows in her parents' living room showed the gauzy drapes fluttering back into place, meaning they'd already been spotted. Too late to turn around and head back to the hotel. If they didn't go into the house soon, her family would send a search party out to retrieve them.

Ayanna's chest pinched and she resisted the urge to take Max's hand. They were friendly now, or at least friendlier than they'd been at the beginning of this, but she didn't want him getting the wrong idea. She'd been specific with her mother as well, when she'd called to tell her to expect her plus one. This wasn't a romantic thing. It was just a nice gesture from one person to another. No one should be alone on the holidays, even if they didn't celebrate. And, sure, Max was a hottie, no two ways about that, but Ayanna had things well in control now regarding her errant sexy thoughts about him. Today was a meal shared with a friend. With her family.

Who were nosy as all get out and now stood on the porch craning their necks, trying to get a better look at the guy she'd brought to Thanksgiving and... *Ugh.*

With a sigh, Ayanna undid her seatbelt, turning slightly to face Max in the passenger seat. "They're probably going to ask you lots of questions, but don't feel like you have to share anything you don't want to, okay?"

"I wouldn't want to be rude," he said, peering out the windshield at her brother Brandon, who had a beer in one hand and a blue and green foam finger that said "Seahawks Number One Fan" on the other. "They're into football, huh?"

"Yeah." Her sister Clarissa stepped out from behind Brandon in her favorite player's jersey and a Seahawks logo temporary tattoo displayed on one cheek. "It's a tradition around here. Do you watch?"

"Not really." Max frowned and sank back in his seat. "Usually I'm working."

"Oh. Well..." She grabbed her purse. "At least I got you out of the suite today. And my mom's food is excellent. Maybe you guys can swap recipes."

"Maybe." His eyes widened slightly.

She checked her makeup in the mirror then pulled out a tube of lip balm to slick some on. "I'm sure you'll be fine." She tossed her lip balm back in her bag then zipped it up. "Ready?"

"Ready."

Ayanna gripped the handles of her purse tightly, more on edge than she cared to admit. She was probably overreacting and her family might very well ignore Max after the introductions were made, but after the whole debacle with Will and the endless litanies of *I told you so* from her siblings, followed by them gathering the wagons around her in support, she wasn't sure, especially since he was the first man she'd brought home since the breakup, date or not.

Besides, she liked Max, more than she had liked anyone in a while. After getting past their initial rocky start and moving into the suite with him, they'd actually discovered they had a lot in common. Both of them were hard workers, both of them loved to watch science documentaries on TV and both of them thought avocados were icky. She didn't want him to feel uncomfortable or out of place today.

Honestly, it had been a long time since she'd found someone she clicked so well with personality-wise in such a short time. Not even Will had meshed into her life so well, especially after he'd started taking her for granted then nitpicking every little thing she did. It would've been almost scary how much she synched with Max Granger if it wasn't for the fact all this was only temporary. As long as she remembered he'd be gone after the King's case was done, she was fine. She flashed him what she hoped was a confident smile. "Okay. Let's get inside before they come over here and drag us out."

He exhaled hard through his nose then turned away to stare out the window beside him, his dark brows drawing together, looking as anxious as she felt. Poor guy. "Okay. I haven't spent time with a family on Thanksgiving since my wife was around."

This time she couldn't resist touching him. His hand felt warm and soft beneath hers. "Losing someone you care for is terrible, and especially hard around this time of year. But I'm glad you're here."

Their gazes locked and the moment stretched tautly between them. Finally, Max gave a small nod, his broad shoulders relaxing beneath the navy-blue sweater he'd worn over a black T-shirt and jeans. He frowned down at her hand covering his. "Is it just the breakup that's making you nervous today?"

"It's just hard, being here. My mom depends on me more than my siblings and I feel like I need to take care of everyone, make sure they're comfortable and happy before I can enjoy myself. Guess it's a holdover from when I used to babysit them when we were younger," she said, sitting back in her own seat to stare out the windshield as truth swelled inside her.

"Don't get me wrong. I love my family. It would just be nice to not have to worry about everyone else all the time." She darted a quick look at him, realizing how that must sound. "Not that I'm complaining. I love my family. I just… I don't know." She shook her head and gave a small shrug. "Anyway, enough about that. My dad's a retired high school history teacher. He'll talk your ear off with long stories about the civil war and the Praetorian Guard, his two favorite subjects. And my mom's a retired ER nurse who's seen and done it all. There isn't a boundary she's afraid to cross when it comes to finding out what she wants to know.

"Then there's James. His partner David is in tech, but he won't be here today. And my other brother Brandon." She pointed out the window at them all, still standing on the porch. "And my sisters Tonya, LaTasha and

Clarissa. We're all pretty close." She finally stopped babbling and just sat there.

Max seemed to take that in for a moment. "I guess the holidays aren't easy for you either, huh?"

"Nope." She laughed, the sound forced and brittle. "It's all fine, though."

"Hmm." Max gave her fingers a gentle squeeze and damn if those nerve endings of hers didn't sizzle again, despite her wishes. Her breath caught and her mouth dried. If he noticed the same rush, he didn't show it. Max just smiled, small and sweet. "Well, in case I forget to say it later, thank you for inviting me. I look forward to meeting Clan Franklin."

She met his eyes again and their gazes snagged, held, the space between them crackling with possibilities.

Ayanna wasn't sure which of them leaned closer first, but then Max licked his lips and she tracked the tiny movement, imagining how his mouth might feel, how his tongue might lick her in all the right spots, how...

Knock, knock, knock.

Startled, Ayanna spun to see Brandon's face pressed to the driver's side window. Dazed, she pressed the button to lower it, hoping her face didn't look as hot as it felt. Thankfully, her brother didn't mention it.

"You guys gonna sit out here all day or come inside?" He raised a brow at her, then glanced at Max as if sizing him up. "Mom said she needs help in the kitchen."

"Right," Ayanna said, the word emerging breathier than she intended. Duty called. As always. She waited until her brother went back inside before closing the window then hazarding a glance over at Max, who'd remained silent. "Are we doing this?"

Tiny patches of crimson dotted his high cheekbones and his Adam's apple bobbed as he swallowed. "Yep. Let's do it."

Max entered the house already feeling off-kilter after their almost-kiss in the car. Now, confronted with hugs and kisses and questions from people he barely knew, to say he was overwhelmed was the understatement of the century.

Still, it wasn't as unpleasant as he'd expected, even when Ayanna disappeared into the kitchen with her mother, presumably to help with dinner and probably talk about him. In fact, as they all gathered around a huge dining room table laden with every kind of food imaginable, from roast turkey and dressing to three kinds of potatoes—mashed, sweet, and baked—along with corn, carrots, green bean casserole, collard greens, fried okra, and a large crockpot full of homemade macaroni and cheese, Max felt something he hadn't felt in a long time. Included. Which was crazy, since he'd just met these people, but there it was. Everything was delicious too, just like Ayanna had promised. He made a mental note to ask her mother for several recipes before they left.

"So, a neurosurgeon, eh?" Ayanna's father said from where he sat at the end of the long dining table. "Ever work with war veterans? There's a lot of documentation about head injuries during the civil war."

"Dad!" Ayanna said from beside Max, placing her hand on his forearm. The warmth of her touch felt much nicer than he cared to admit. "Please, he just got here. Plus, this is his day off. I'm sure Max doesn't want to talk about work stuff today."

"It's fine," Max said, swallowing another bit of succulent turkey and dressing. Growing up, his nannies had always had holiday dinners delivered from a local restaurant. The food had been fine, but nothing like all this homemade fare. His mother had never cooked. She'd been too busy traveling or working out the specifics of a new procedure.

He'd already cleared one plate of food and gone back for second helpings of everything, not missing the way Ayanna's mother kept a watchful eye on him, her smile widening the more he ate. He finished dishing up more mac and cheese and candied sweet potatoes, then took a swig of water. Ayanna didn't know it, but he was a bit of a civil war buff himself. "I did know, Mr. Franklin. In fact, my paper for one of my classes in med school was on battlefield treatments of closed head injuries during that time period."

"Interesting!" Her father smiled beneath his white mustache. The knot of tension between Max's shoulder blades eased a tad. "We'll talk after dinner then, son. And, please, call me Harry."

Max felt like he'd just won a huge prize, though he couldn't say exactly why. After all, this was just one meal, one day. He probably wouldn't see these people again after he left Seattle. Still, the thought of being accepted by Ayanna's family banished his shadows for a while.

"Thank you, Harry," Max said, then turned to Ayanna's mother. "And thank you, Mrs. Franklin, for having me today. Everything is delicious and your home is beautiful. I like to cook a fair bit myself. Perhaps we can talk food later, if you don't mind."

"My, my. Gotta love a man who's confident in the kitchen." The older woman beamed then gave her oldest daughter a pointed look. Max could certainly see where Ayanna got her beauty from. Their smiles were so similar it caused Max's chest to tighten. "And thank you for the compliments. Please, call me Narissa. We can absolutely talk turkey today. And you're always welcome in our home, Max. Any friend of my daughter's is a friend of ours too." Max didn't miss the unspoken hint of warning in her tone, though.

Unless you hurt Ayanna, then all bets are off.

He thought about her ex's actions and his dislike for the man grew, even though they'd never met. He and Ayanna were still getting to know each other, but from what Max had seen so far she was a wonderful woman. Smart, funny, hard-working, loyal. Her ex must've been an idiot to take her for granted then run out on her the way he had.

"Maybe after dinner Ayanna can give you a full tour of the place," Narissa said, breaking Max out of his thoughts. Then she reached over and took her husband's hand, the affection between them clear. "Harry and I built this place when Ayanna was just a baby. Back then real estate prices around here were more reasonable. We were lucky to get in before the big housing boom in Seattle, when we could still afford this land on a nurse's and teacher's salaries."

"Dude," Brandon said to Max from across the table, cutting his mom off. "Can you take a look at my shoulder later? I pulled something shooting hoops last month and my hand keeps tingling at night when I'm trying to sleep."

"Seriously, Bran?" Ayanna tossed her napkin on the table, giving her brother a look. "Which part of he's not working today did you not understand?"

Max stifled a laugh and stared down at his food. Ayanna was cute when she was feisty, which was basically all the time.

Wait. What?

The thought stopped him short. He had no business thinking of Ayanna like that, especially now that they were sharing the suite. Yes, they'd spent more time together since Sunday and he knew more about her—like how she liked her eggs and what perfume she wore and how she had to have socks on at night in order to sleep. That wasn't an invitation to cross an invisible line from friendship to something more. In fact, if anything, that moment in the car earlier when they'd almost kissed should've sent him fleeing far and fast in the opposite direction. He didn't want to get involved romantically ever again. Didn't want to open himself up to that kind of vulnerability and pain. He was perfectly happy in his self-imposed workaholic isolation.

Aren't I?

He certainly had been when he'd arrived here in Seattle. Now, though, sitting in a raucous dining room filled with family and laughter and food, he wasn't so sure. Brandon was still looking at him expectantly from across the table and Max nodded. "Sure, I can take a look at your shoulder. My specialty is the brain, but the nervous system is the nervous system."

Max felt Ayanna's stare tingling on his skin so he focused on finishing the last of his mashed potatoes and gravy instead of looking at her for fear she might see the conflicting emotions in his eyes—joy, fear, hope, hesitation. Luckily, the conversation picked up again and continued around him as he finished his food then pushed away his empty plate. Stomach full and suddenly feeling in need of a nap, he took a deep breath then sat back, careful to keep his arms close to his sides to avoid brushing against Ayanna again. For some reason, he was having even more trouble battling his deepening attraction to her. He didn't want to deal with that right now, though, just wanted to enjoy what was left of today.

"All right, then," Narissa said, standing to begin clearing away the dishes. "Kids, help your mama clear this table, then we've got pumpkin pie for dessert." Ayanna started to get up, along with her siblings, but her mother stopped her. "Not you, Ayanna. You take your Max and show him the rest of Casa Franklin."

"He's not my Max, Mom," Ayanna said, giving him an apologetic side glance. "I told you we're just working together while he's in town. Are you sure you don't want my help? I'm usually your go-to gal."

"You usually don't have a guest with you either, honey," Narissa said, shaking her head. "I know you like to take care of everyone else, but let us take care of you today, okay? Now, go show Max around our house." She stopped in the hallway through the doorway into the kitchen, arms laden with dirty dishes, and glanced back at Ayanna with a stern look. "And don't get any ideas about rushing through things to hurry back down here to take over. We will survive without you, honey. I don't want to see either of you in my kitchen until it's time for pie. Go on. The rest of you, dish duty. Now."

Her siblings whined and grumbled, but not one of them refused their momma. They all knew better.

Max pushed to his feet beside Ayanna, taking in her somewhat shocked expression. "Sounds like she means business."

"I guess she does." Ayanna moved out behind her chair then pushed it in before gesturing for him to proceed her out of the open dining room. "After you."

"You looked surprised she's letting you out of dish duty," he joked as they headed back toward the front of the house.

"I am," Ayanna said, giving him a half-grin. "It's like winning the lottery or something. You must be good luck."

Warmth spread from his core to his extremities and he found himself grinning along with her. "Well, I don't know about that, but I'll take it."

They started back at the foyer, with its pickled pine floors and high cathedral ceiling. A staircase sat back against the far wall and above a loft overlooked the whole area.

The house overall was bright and open and inviting and reminded Max of the home he and Laura had bought in Jericho, Long Island, when he'd been working regularly out of Manhattan. It had been a craftsmen-style too, though not nearly as large as this home. Then again, it had just been the two of them.

"See that loft up there?" Ayanna pointed to the second floor. "James and Brandon jumped off there one time after seeing *Iron Man*. Good thing they dragged the couch cushions out here first to break their fall. I thought Mom was going to kill them herself after that."

"I bet," Max said, following her into the living room to stand before said couch. This room too was light and airy, decorated in shades of light grays and blues. One wall was taken up by windows and the other held a large flat-screen TV. Recessed lighting in the ceiling, along with speakers and deep, overstuffed furniture marked this as a home theater as well as a place for guests to gather. Next they visited a small office that belonged to her father before heading upstairs to the loft.

From up here the noise and laughter of her family were muted, and it seemed like they were in their own tiny world. Ayanna looked over the railing then turned to him. "Did you enjoy dinner?"

"I did. I like your family." He was surprised to find he meant it. Honestly, today was the first time in recent memory that he'd been able to just relax. Being here with Ayanna and her family had been nice and comfortable, and for that he was grateful. "Today's been kind of wonderful, actually."

"Yeah?" She smiled back at him and tilted her head. His heart tripped. They stared at each other for a moment and the same invisible cord that had connected them in the car returned, drawing them closer, closer, until Ayanna cleared her throat and moved away to continue the tour, saying under her breath, "That's enough of that."

She showed him the master bedroom and bath, a small library with a reading nook, and a guest bath followed by several smaller bedrooms, pointing out which had belonged to her siblings, before stopping at one room in the corner. "And this used to be my old bedroom."

He stepped inside, taking in the pastel purple walls and shiny wood floors, the twin bed and the picture hanging above it with a quote in white, "I love you, a bushel and a peck."

"Yeah." Ayanna snorted. "My mom bought

it at a flea market. She used to sing me that song when I was little."

Max frowned. "Uh, don't think I've heard that one."

"Really?" She started to sing. At his befuddled look, she laughed. "Well, anyway, it was her favorite song to sing at night when I couldn't sleep. So when she found this at the flea market, she had to have it."

"That's sweet." He studied some framed photos on the wall showing Ayanna when she'd been younger. Still cute. There was one of her in a cheerleading uniform and one in a ballet tutu. Another of her and a group of other little girls selling cookies. A bittersweet pang stabbed between his ribs. "Looks like you were involved in a lot of activities growing up. The only thing my parents allowed me to participate in were academic clubs. Science, math, things like that. And even then it was the nannies who shuttled me around."

"Nannies?" Ayanna frowned. "You must've been super rich growing up."

"No." Max turned away, shame and defensiveness searing his throat. "My parents were always working and couldn't be home with me, so they hired people. Good thing they only had one child to deal with."

Ayanna walked over and placed her hand on his arm again, the heat of her touch soothing. "That must've been really lonely for you. I'm sorry."

"It was fine." He shifted away, resisting the urge to take her hand again. "They weren't bad parents, just busy. And I never lacked for anything."

"Except love," she whispered, shaking her head. "And connection."

Max took a deep breath then forced a smile, eager to get out of this room that seemed smaller and hotter all of a sudden. "It's in the past. Where to next?"

"That's basically it, I'm afraid." They went back out to the loft and sat on the loveseat against the wall. It was cozy nook, far enough back from the railing that it couldn't be seen from below. Ayanna toed off her shoes and tucked one stockinged foot beneath her, resting her elbow against the back cushion to face him. "There's a deck out back, but since it's raining now, we should probably wait on that."

"Agreed." He stifled a yawn. Between all the food he'd eaten and the ease of being around Ayanna and her family today, he felt sleepy. After pushing himself non-stop for the past two years since his wife's death, it was a welcome, unexpected relief. "Thank you for the tour."

"Thank you for coming." She'd gone with jeans and a sweater, the same as him, though hers was a light pink color and fuzzy. He wondered if it felt as soft as it looked and damn if that didn't set the blood singing in his veins again. Guard down and unable to resist, he reached over and took her hand, the way he'd been wanting to for what felt like forever. Her dark eyes widened and her lips parted slightly as he leaned in once more until her warm breath fanned his face. Max wasn't sure what he was doing, only that it felt necessary, like if he didn't kiss her right then, he'd be missing out on something precious. All the guilt, all the anger, all the darkness that had haunted him disappeared in that moment until there was only now, only them, only this kiss.

He half expected her to pull away again, but this time she didn't. Time seemed to slow. Then his lips brushed hers and the rest of the world fell away. Her breath caught and he pulled back. A dull voice in the back of his head warned him to be careful, to slow down, this was all too much too soon. But then Max saw those soft lips of hers parted and ready and he was lost.

His mouth brushed hers again and Ayanna groaned low in her throat. Her hand slid into the hair at the nape of his neck, holding him close, pulling him tighter against her as if she felt the same rush, the same urgency. She gasped and he took advantage, sweeping his tongue inside to taste her—cinnamon from the sweet potatoes and decadent temptation—and he couldn't get enough. It had been too long since he'd held someone close, since he'd felt their heart race alongside his, since he'd heard their tiny mewls of need, since…

The sound of a clearing throat had them springing apart fast.

Max sat back, blinking hard as Ayanna ran a flustered hand through her hair. She coughed and scowled over at her other brother, James. "What is it?"

"Pie's ready," he said, giving them each a coy look, smirking. "But seems like you two are already having your own special kind of dessert."

"Shut up." Ayanna stood and smoothed the front of her sweater. "Tell Mom we'll be right down."

"Oh, I'll tell her all right." He snickered then started back downstairs, pulling out his phone. "Wait until David hears about this…"

Face flushed, Ayanna turned back to Max. "Sorry. Nosy, like I told you."

"They care about you, that's all." Except as he stood and followed her back down the stairs, all he could think about was the fact that he'd just kissed Ayanna Franklin, the woman he'd sworn not to, and he couldn't quite wrap his head around it. Max wasn't impulsive. He wasn't emotional.

And yet, with Ayanna, *he was*. In fact, his heart was still racing and his lips still tingled from their encounter.

They returned to the dining room and ate pie, but Max could've been chewing plywood for all he tasted it. Each time he licked his lips he'd swear he still tasted Ayanna, and every time her family looked at him, it seemed like they knew exactly what they'd been up to on that loveseat upstairs. Or maybe that was his own conscience. He was acting like an idiot, pure and simple. He'd gone too long denying his needs, that had to be it.

Logic ruled him most of the time and while that suited him fine, perhaps he'd gone too overboard with it and now he'd acted out because of it. Yes, that made sense. What didn't make sense, though, was the pull he felt to Ayanna even now, maybe more so since their kiss. The yearning to hold her and touch her and taste her that drowned out everything else. For a man who lived by his mind and not his emotions, it made him question everything.

The next few hours passed in a blur. Max watched sports with her family without paying much attention. Checked her brother's shoulder and advised him to see his family doctor for an X-ray and possibly PT. Then the afternoon was gone and it was time to go. He and Ayanna said their goodbyes and he got more hugs and kisses from her family, plus handwritten recipes from Narissa. By the time they were back in her SUV and heading for the hotel, his thoughts were jumbled worse than the traffic jam they ran into on the highway. The conflict inside him had reached a crescendo and he needed answers. Needed clarity. Needed to figure out a way beyond this mess and back to the logical world he loved. "Listen, about what happened in the loft—"

"Forget it, okay?" Ayanna said, not looking at him, seemingly as disturbed as he was by their kiss. "Don't mention it again. It's better that way."

Right. Good. Forget about it. That made sense. He nodded then stared out the window beside him. Forgetting it was the best possible thing they could do. The kiss had been a mistake. An aberration. They should both move on and never look back again.

But as they drove through downtown Seattle, all Max could seem to think about now was Ayanna, for better or worse.

CHAPTER EIGHT

"No, I'm sorry. We have no information to report about the accident victims from last week," Ayanna said to the reporter on the other end of the line. She'd been fielding calls, along with her staff, for most of the day and yet they still kept coming in. "Yes, that's an official statement. Thank you."

She hung up then covered her face with her hands. It was nearly four o'clock and she'd gotten almost nothing accomplished on her to-do list for the ball. Then again, her lack of productivity could also have had something to do with the fact she'd slept like crap the night before. Tossing and turning and replaying that stupid kiss with Max over and over in her head.

Why exactly she'd let him kiss her, Ayanna wasn't sure. But she was certain it wouldn't be happening again. For one, getting involved with him was one more complication she did not need right now. Sure, Max was wonderful. Yes, her family had taken to him like a polar bear to snow. In fact, they'd been blowing up her cellphone with texts all day. But neither of those things were good reasons to go all gaga over the guy.

Right?

She put her head down atop her arms on her desk. If only she could rely on what her instincts were telling her—that Max wasn't like Will, that he appreciated her, that he understood her in a way Will never had—but she couldn't. Even now, months after the breakup, her ability to trust herself was still shredded. Shredded by the hurt. The embarrassment. The stupidity of not knowing what she should've seen right in front of her face.

Ayanna groaned and squeezed her eyes shut. No. She couldn't go through that again. Will's betrayal had made her doubt herself. Doubt her instincts about people. And if she couldn't trust herself to make good choices about who to let into her life, who's to say letting Max in wouldn't be a mistake too?

Her head hurt and her heart ached. Not that she needed to worry about things going too far with Max because they'd both agreed to forget all about that kiss last night. It was over. Done.

Except each time she closed her eyes, images of them on the loveseat had filled her head.

She sat back and sighed. This was what her life had become these days. Stolen kisses and forbidden fumbles. The fact she knew Max was just down the hall from her in his office hadn't helped either.

A knock sounded on the door and she straightened, smoothing her hair before calling, "Come in."

"Hey." The man in question stuck his head into her office, setting her traitorous pulse fluttering again. "Are we still leaving at five?"

"Uh…" At the sight of him, her usual gift of the gab went right out the window. Man, she was in serious trouble here. To distract herself, she frowned down at her phone instead of drooling over him, and pulled up the calendar, only to wince. "Oops. Can we do four-thirty instead? I need to make a stop for the ball planning on the way to the hotel, if you don't mind."

Max pulled out his own phone to check, the overhead lights revealing dark shadows beneath his eyes, suggesting maybe she hadn't been the only one with kiss-induced insomnia last night. The thought made her feel slightly better, for reasons she didn't want to analyze. "Um, yeah. Four-thirty should be doable for me. I've got documentation and follow-ups to get done on a couple of cases, then I should be able to leave early. I'll come back here when I'm ready."

"Sounds good." He left and she released her pent-up breath. Things between them had seemed normal just then. Maybe too normal. Or maybe she was reading too much into this because that's what she did. Overanalyzed everything to try and stay two steps ahead of everyone else. Anticipating their wants and needs. Putting those possible outcomes before her own agenda. And…

Oh, God. She covered her face again. Max was right. She did try to fix everything. She was all for self-actualization but, man, couldn't a girl catch a break for once? She frowned at the Charlie Brown Christmas tree on her desk, its one red ornament drooping, just like her mood. Even her family had seemed to treat her differently when Max was around, not expecting her to take care of all their problems for once, just letting her enjoy her day. It had been weird and wonderful and completely discombobulating.

Tired and irritable, she did her best to get back to work on the menus for the ball. The errand she'd mentioned to Max involved the dessert. Considering he was a self-proclaimed foodie, she thought she might as well put his skills to the test by picking out the dessert for the ball. Now, if she could just make up her mind on the rest of the food, she'd be all set. They were down to the wire, with less than two weeks left until the fundraiser, and if she didn't finalize the catering menu soon, they'd end up having cheese and crackers from the local grocery store. Not exactly a good way to impress her new bosses or the donors.

The next thirty minutes dragged by in another tangle of phone calls and budgets and descriptions of gourmet dishes that either sounded way too fancy or way too expensive for what she needed. One of the keys to a successful event was giving people the same, but different. Whacky designer dishes might seem like a great idea on paper, but if no one knew what they were eating, it wouldn't go down well—literally or figuratively. Finally, she'd narrowed the choices down to a few items and made notes to request them from the kitchens at the Polar Club to sample before placing her final order. Maybe Max could help her with those as well.

And speaking of Max, he tapped on her

door at that moment to let her know he was ready.

Perfect.

She gathered her bag and phone then shut down her computer and said goodbye to her staff before heading out of her office to meet Max in the hall by the elevators.

He'd changed out of scrubs into khakis and a soft-looking black turtleneck. Her fingertips itched with a weird urge to stroke his chest and see if he felt as solid and warm as she remembered from the day before. Ayanna stopped herself clenching the handles of her brown leather satchel and stared straight ahead at the elevator doors.

Get a grip, girl.

The elevator dinged and he held the door for her to board first. As she passed him, Ayanna caught a hint of sandalwood and cedar soap on his skin. And just like that all her good intentions fell by the wayside. Goosebumps of awareness rose on her arms and the backs of her knees buzzed with adrenaline. Memories of his mouth on hers, the sweep of his tongue, the flavor of salt and sweetness in his kisses swamped her.

Oh, boy. This was bad. So, so bad. What if she'd read it all wrong? What if Max wasn't the good guy she thought he was? What if he couldn't be trusted, just like Will? What if...?

"Where are we going?" Max asked, his words jarring her out of her downward spiral. "On that ball-related errand you mentioned."

"Oh." She gathered her red trench coat closer around her like a shield. "A local bakery. I thought you could help me choose the dessert for the evening." At his surprised look, she smiled. "What? You said you wanted to help, and I could use a second set of taste buds to make sure I'm picking out the right one."

"Okay."

"And don't worry about cooking dinner tonight. I'll order in samples of the dinner menu selections for us to try."

"Sounds good." Max gave a curt nod. "It's been quite a day and cake makes everything better."

"Amen to that," she said, then stopped herself. "Sorry. Nothing new with the King, I hope?"

"No. His condition is still the same." He didn't elaborate and that was good. HIPAA laws were there for a reason, namely to protect patient privacy. "Just hectic."

The elevator dinged and the doors slid open on the first floor. They walked outside and across the street to her car. Max got in and buckled his seatbelt while Ayanna climbed in behind the wheel and tossed her bag on the backseat.

"Is this the same place I went to the other day for lunch?" Max asked. "The Thunderbird Café?"

"No. Different place. This one specializes in cakes and they do some really innovative things with flavor profiles, so I'm excited to check it out. They were rated as the top bakery in Seattle by one of the local food magazines too. Figured having them do our desserts for the gala might score me some bonus points with the big money donors."

"Good thinking." Max grinned then faced front again, yawning. "Man, I'm beat."

"Me too," she said, as they headed through the streets of Seattle toward Seahawk Sweets and Confections, glad the awkwardness had abated for the time being. They chatted about nothing in particular. He told her about a couple of consults he'd done in the ER—a car accident victim and a schoolteacher who'd collapsed at work—and they both steered clear of the subject of their kiss the previous evening, thank goodness.

Finally, they arrived at the bakery and she pulled into a spot alongside the brick building on Carlton Avenue then cut the engine. Ayanna checked her watch and grabbed her purse, feeling like she'd dodged a bullet. "Here we are. Let's get inside before we're late."

"First we have our peach bourbon cake," the owner, a woman in her mid-thirties with glasses and a thunderbird tattoo on her arm, said half an hour later. "It's made with a ricotta olive oil cake and a bourbon soak. The filling is dark salted caramel and peach, topped with cream cheese frosting."

Max took a bite of his small slice and thought he'd died and gone to heaven. Sweet and boozy with just a hint of salt from the filling. He glanced over at Ayanna beside him for her reaction then and oops. Big mistake. He'd been doing so well too, avoiding thinking about her lips and all. But one look at her, her eyes closed and head tipped back in ecstasy, and boom. His blood pumped and his heart galloped like a racehorse at the Derby. He wiped his damp palms on the legs of his pants and did his best to ignore her throaty little moan.

No. No, no, no.

This wasn't him. He wasn't ruled by his emotions. He didn't lead with his heart.

Mind out of the gutter, head in the game. He was here to help Ayanna pick a cake for the ball. That was all. Now, if someone could just convey that message to his tightening body, he'd be all set.

Thankfully, Ayanna didn't seem notice his raging response. "What do you think?"

I think I'd like to continue where we left off last night with that kiss...

Dammit. He bit back the words, coughing then sipping water from the plastic cup the owner had set in front of each of them to cover it. "This one's marvelous," he said, his words gruffer than normal from the testosterone tearing through his body. He cleared his throat and tried again. "But we should try them all first before deciding."

"Agreed."

The owner took their plates away to replace them with new slices of cake. This new one had dark chocolate frosting and a slight hint of pine. Intrigued, Max took a bite, glad for a distraction from the adorable way Ayanna was tilting her head as she concentrated. It was one of things he loved about her.

Love?

His thoughts screeched to a halt while

Ayanna asked the owner, "And what's this one?"

"This is our PNW chocolate. Dark chocolate cake infused with pine oil and porter beer then covered with a semi-sweet chocolate ganache also flavored with pine."

Max only half heard that, his mind still churning over the fact he'd used the L-word, even casually, where Ayanna was concerned. He liked her, yes, way more than he probably should, but he had no business going further than that. They were friends. Nothing more.

Friends who kissed.

He scowled and chewed his bite of cake and did his best to concentrate on the unique flavor profile instead of his memories of how Ayanna had tasted—like cinnamon and spice and everything nice. Frowning, he focused his attention on his taste buds. There was a slight bitterness to this cake, offset by the sweeter ganache frosting. The addition of pine and porter balanced all the flavors out with a brightness he'd never thought possible. He dug it. Based on Ayanna's reaction, however, she didn't.

"Gotta say it's not my favorite." She pushed her plate away without another bite. "I love chocolate, but the pine reminds me too much of my mom's floor cleaner. Sorry."

"Not at all." The owner laughed. "It's an acquired taste. Let's move on to the last one, shall we?" She placed a new small slice in front of each of them, this one with a dark gray marbled frosting. "We call this one London Fog. Earl Grey tea infused cake soaked in honey and Earl Grey syrup, bergamot mascarpone cream filling and topped with cream cheese frosting. It's our newest creation and the one I'm most proud of."

Ayanna took a bite and her dark eyes widened. She quickly gobbled down a second and third bite. "Wow. I love this one."

Max had to agree. The hint of tea flavor wasn't overpowering, as he'd feared. Instead, the bergamot and mascarpone cream filling balanced it out to perfection. The addition of the slight tang from the cream cheese frosting was a great finish to a glorious cake. He polished off his slice too. "I vote this one."

"I think we have a winner." Ayanna grinned. "Our ball is on the evening of December twelfth at the Polar Club. We'll need to have enough to serve two hundred. Is that possible?"

The owner opened a binder and leafed through a few pages. "Yes. We should be able to accommodate that, though you just made it in under the wire."

"Should you consider doing half and half?" Max asked, pointing to one of the vegan cakes they'd sampled earlier. "Just in case some donors have food allergies or dietary preferences."

"Oh, good idea." Ayanna nodded. "Sorry. I've had so much on my mind I didn't think of that. Yes. Can I change the order to half London Fog cake and half the vegan option, please? Honestly, that vegan cake is so tasty, I didn't even miss the eggs and butter."

"Sure." The owner made a few more notes then wrote up the paperwork. "Anything else? If you change your mind after tonight, there's a fifteen percent surcharge."

"Nope. We're good." Ayanna signed off and handed the woman her corporate credit card.

Once that was done, they went back outside. Dusk had settled in and the streetlights gave an orange glow as they returned to her vehicle. Ayanna got in then started the car before looking over at him as he buckled his seatbelt. "Thanks for your help in there."

"No problem." He chuckled. "I mean, eating gourmet cake is a hardship, but I'm willing to suffer."

"Right." Her smile beamed through the darkness, and that darned connection, the one he'd tried so hard to avoid, tugged a little tighter in his gut. "And good catch on the vegan thing," Ayanna said. "It could've cost me a lot more tomorrow to change the order."

"No problem," he said, resisting the urge to brush back the curls that had fallen across her cheek. "Guess we make a pretty good team, huh?"

"Yes, we do." She swallowed hard, heat flickering through her gaze, so fast he would've missed it if he hadn't been concentrating on her so intently. Her breath hitched and his pulse stumbled. Then Ayanna faced front again, signaling then pulling out of their parking spot to merge into traffic. "Now on to those dinner samples at the hotel."

"Yep." Max watched the passing scenery, knowing avoidance when he saw it. Seemed they were both becoming experts in it these days.

"Uh, will Ohio do?" a familiar male voice said from below, and Ayanna froze. She glanced down to see Max holding up a brightly painted glass globe with the name "Justin" scrawled in red and green across the middle with rainbow glitter around the edges. Each child was encouraged to make the ornament their own. "It looks like it would fit the space you're filling."

"It does. Thanks. What are you doing here?" she asked, taking it from him to hang on the branch she'd chosen. He was right. It fit perfectly. Ayanna climbed down and matched his grin with one of her own. "No patients this afternoon?"

"Finished my rounds early." He took her arm to steady her as she slipped her shoes back on then walked across the atrium with her to see how the trees looked from a distance. "A day without many neurological emergencies is both rare and much appreciated."

"I bet." She squinted at the tree, searching for any bare spots or clumps of decorations. The silver and gold garlands caught the sunlight filtering in through the glass atrium above and twinkled nearly as brightly as the white fairy lights strung through the branches. People riding up and down the es-

CHAPTER NINE

"TODD, CAN YOU hand me another ornament, please?" Ayanna said from the top of a ladder in the hospital's glass-walled atrium. Beside her was a towering artificial spruce. It was a yearly tradition here at Seattle General now that December first had arrived, though the addition of the handmade ornaments from childhood cancer patients around the country was new, as were the gifts being left beneath the tree by staff to give to be distributed in the children's wards.

Both ideas had been Ayanna's, to help boost the hospital's standing as one of the city's top philanthropic organizations. So far, the tree and the gifts were proving immensely popular, with many people stopping to take photos, even though the final decorations were only now being put up. "How about one from Indiana? I don't think that state's represented here yet."

calators behind the tree seemed appropriately awed, she noted. However, there was one area where the décor wasn't quite balanced.

Ayanna held up a finger to stop Max's continued explanation about his day, then called across the space, "Hey, Todd? Can you please spread out those ornaments a bit more so they're evenly spaced? No. Not there. A bit more to the left and up about three branches. Yes! Good. Thanks."

Satisfied, she turned back to Max. "Are you ready to go now? I've got some time yet until things are done here in the lobby. We still need to hang the mistletoe and add lights and garland to the rest of the room." She narrowed her gaze on him. "Don't suppose you'd want to help, would you?"

"Eh, I don't want to get in the way," Max said. "I'm sure I can find something to occupy my time until you're ready to leave."

Ayanna opened her mouth to tell him he wouldn't be in the way at all but was cut off by the sound of shattering glass. Her attention snapped back to the tree again, where Todd gave her a sheepish look.

"Sorry, boss," he said. "At least it wasn't one of the handmade ones. Just a glass icicle from the store."

"Be careful," Ayanna called back, shaking her head before looking at Max once more.

He was still scowling at Todd and the tree. "He's doing that wrong."

"Huh?" She scrunched her nose and glanced back at her staffer. "How can you hang ornaments wrong?"

"There's a proper way to loop the wires around the branches for maximum support and safety. Plus, the ratios are all wrong."

"Ratios? Seriously?" Ayanna raised a brow. "Not to sound clichéd, but this isn't brain surgery, Max."

"Funny." He rolled his eyes then placed his hands on her shoulders to turn her around to face the tree again, keeping her directly in front of him. Warmth from his touch penetrated her black blazer, making her knees wobble and her blood sizzle. Part of her brain told Ayanna to step away from temptation, but damn if she could get her feet to move. Max reached past her to point at where Todd was working. His forearm brushed her ear and her core gave a tiny squeeze of want before she could stop it.

"Squint. See how the sizes are too similar on the right-hand side and the colors are all the same in that area, making the composition unbalanced? Mixing them up helps the overall design and keeps it looking fresh."

Ayanna opened her mouth to make another snarky comment but, man. He was right again. "For a guy who hates Christmas, you sure seem to know a lot about it. Your wife must've trained you well."

The minute the words were out, she wished she could take them back. What a stupid, insensitive thing for her to say, knowing what he'd been through, losing his wife. She was the gal who always knew the right words to say, but with Max they always seemed to come out wrong. He stepped away and she missed the heat of him immediately. Ayanna looked back over her shoulder. "I'm sorry. I didn't mean to—"

"No. It's fine." His remote expression said otherwise. "I'm going to go back up to my office to finish a few things. I'll meet you by the elevators at six as planned."

Ayanna watched him walk away, the attraction inside her quickly shifting to a need to atone. Dammit. Things between them had finally settled back into a nice, normal rhythm after their mistaken kiss and then she had to go and ruin things by blurting out what she had.

And, sure, maybe she still couldn't seem

to forget about what had happened in her parents' loft and move on, but that was her problem, not his. She liked Max. Way more than she should, but again it was her issue to deal with. She liked talking with him, spending time with him, having him help her with the ball prep. He'd been way more assistance than she'd ever thought possible and she didn't like to see him unhappy, especially because of her.

She wanted him to smile. Wanted to see him relaxed and joyful. Not because she was coming to care for him in ways that had nothing to do with friendship. She was fixer, that was all. And being around him so much brought out her caretaker side.

And maybe if you tell yourself that enough times it'll make it true.

Sighing, she went over to help Todd redistribute the decorations based on Max's advice.

Two hours later, the tree and the rest of the lobby looked amazing and Ayanna felt worse than ever about her flippant comment to Max. She wanted to do something to make it up to him but wasn't sure what. She couldn't cook. That was Max's area. Obviously design wasn't her forte either, since he'd just bested her there too. By the time she made it back to her office, Ayanna began to wonder if there was anything Max Granger wasn't good at. Then Wham's "Last Christmas" came on the overhead sound system and a deep, off-key male voice bellowed down the hall from the direction of his office and… *Whoa!* Yeah. That was awful. Like am angry cat caught in a shower drain. Ayanna cringed on Max's behalf.

Ding! Ding! Ding! We have a winner. The man couldn't carry a tune to save his life.

She stood in the empty hall and stifled her laugh while her ears rang from his sour notes. Good thing the rest of the staff on the floor had cleared out earlier. It was after six, so she and staff from Housekeeping were the only ones there. Finally, the last chorus died away, and Ayanna couldn't resist teasing him any longer. Moving silently down the hall, she pushed open his office door then leaned her shoulder against the wall. "Wow. That was… Wow. Words can't accurately describe what I just heard."

"What?" He swiveled fast in his chair to face her, tiny splotches of crimson dotting his cheekbones. "Uh, sorry. I didn't know you were back. I don't usually sing in front of other people."

"Thank you, Lord." They both cracked up, laughing for a moment before Ayanna set aside the box of leftover decorations she'd carried back with her from the lobby. "I get it, though. I love Wham too."

He bit his lips then shook his head, losing the battle as another bark of laughter escaped him. "You caught me. I guess maybe I don't *entirely* hate Christmas after all. Just parts of it." He shrugged. "Does that make sense?"

"Sure. I mean, I still can't stand the sight of all those bridal shows and spring wedding commercials on TV."

Max winced. "Yeah. I can't imagine."

Ayanna took a deep breath to ward off the usual knot of anger and betrayal that tightened her chest whenever she thought of Will, but for some reason it didn't come. Instead, she just felt hollow. Like her hurt had burned away a hole that was waiting to be refilled. "Listen, I'm sorry again about what I said downstairs."

"Don't worry about it. Really." He ran a hand through his hair, leaving the dark, thick strands spiked atop his head. He looked messy and completely adorable. A tiny quiver of need vibrated through her like a tuning fork and... Uh-oh. Yeah. Whether she wanted to admit it or not, her feelings for

Max Granger had gone way past like and tumbled straight into lust. He stood and grabbed his jacket off the back of his chair. "I'm good."

Yes, you are. She swallowed hard and turned away from the sight of his muscles rippling as he tugged on his coat. "Let me just grab my stuff and we can leave."

Ayanna made a hasty retreat and didn't breathe again until she was alone in her office. Oh, boy. She didn't want to want Max that way. What if he turned out to be a player? The last thing she wanted was to trust the wrong man again and have her heart broken again. Except her heart wasn't on the line this time.

Wasn't it?

"Ready when you are," Max said from her office door, jolting her out of her thoughts.

"Great," Ayanna said with a burst of fake cheerfulness. She pulled on her coat and grabbed her purse, making sure she had her phone before heading back downstairs with him to the parking lot. "Uh, thanks again for your advice on the tree. It really did make a difference."

"You're welcome." He held the door for her in the lobby then followed Ayanna outside into the chilly, damp evening air. Even

though the temperature was above freezing, the breeze blowing in off Puget Sound felt cold enough for snow. "Instead of me cooking tonight, want to stop on the way back to the hotel and pick up some dinner? My treat."

"Oh, I'm not very hungry," she said, the lights of her vehicle blinking as she unlocked the doors using her key fob. Not a lie. Her gut was churning from the unexpected realization that she wanted Max as way more than just a friend. "Besides, I've, uh, got more work to do tonight, so I'll probably just heat up some soup or something later."

"Okay. But no skipping meals," he said, sliding into the seat next to her and giving her a stern look. "We talked about that. Maybe I can call down for room service. Or I think there might still be some leftovers from the menu tasting we did the other day. I know there's some butternut squash ravioli left. Maybe some Caprese salad too."

"That's fine." She could've eaten dust bunnies for all she cared at the moment. Her brain was still stuck on the fact that somehow Max had slipped beneath her defenses and now there didn't seem to be anything she could do about it. She started the car then pulled out of the lot. "I don't need much. Whatever makes you happy."

His expression turned thoughtful as Max stared out the window beside him while she drove. "What makes you happy, Ayanna?"

"Huh?" She looked over at him, her heart in her throat. She felt vulnerable enough where he was concerned without getting into this at the moment. "I'm happy."

"Are you?" His gaze shifted back to her, those gray-green eyes of his far too perceptive for her comfort. "I know it's probably none of my business, but in the short time I've known you, you always seem far more concerned about making other people comfortable than you do about yourself."

She jammed on her turn signal, not looking at him. "Catering to other people's needs is my job."

"Hmm." He exhaled slowly as a few stray snowflakes began to fall and stick to the windshield. "Did you learn that growing up?"

Yes. "No." *Liar.*

Max shifted slightly to rest one elbow on the window ledge, the seatbelt stretching tautly across his broad chest. "You know, part of my job as a surgeon is to figure out why things are the way they are and the best way to correct them. Take the King's tumor. I had that model made so I could see the problem from all angles then decide on the best course of action surgically to remove it all with the least risk possible." He blinked at her. "If only all life's problems were that easy to correct."

"Brain tumors are easy?" Ayanna gave him a skeptical glance, desperately trying to change the subject away from her personal life and failing, if Max's flat stare was any indication.

He took a deep breath and faced the window beside him again, the glass fogging slightly when he exhaled. "It was my fault my wife died."

"What? No." Ayanna slowed for a red light before focusing on him again. "I don't believe that."

"It's true." Max rubbed his hand over his jaw. "She had an aneurysm. I, of all people, should've recognized the symptoms when they started and had her tested. The headaches, the stiffness in her neck, the extreme fatigue. But we were both working so much. Me with my traveling and teaching and her with her OB/GYN practice. She swore to me that it was nothing." He gave a sad snort and scrubbed his hand over his face. "I did exactly what I warn my patients not to do. I ignored the warning signs. As it was, I wasn't even there when she died. I was stuck across town in a lecture and with traffic I didn't arrive at the hospital until she'd already slipped away." He shook his head and scowled at the snow outside. "How ironic is that? The world-renowned neurosurgeon can't even save his own wife."

"Oh, Max." Ayanna reached over to take his hand, only to have the car behind her honk when the light turned green. Cursing under her breath, she accelerated through the intersection then pulled over into a nearby parking lot without paying much attention to the location. "There's no way you could've known what would happen. I'm not a medical professional, but I remember hearing stories from my mom growing up of patients with aneurysms coming into the ER. By nature, they're unpredictable. You can't feel guilty over something you can't control."

"I know that. Logically." He stared down at his hands in his lap. "But knowing it doesn't make it any easier to believe."

"I get it. I do." She put the car into park then leaned back in her seat. "I still don't trust myself after what happened with Will. Looking back, there were so many red flags that things weren't right between us. His secretiveness, the way he gaslighted me into

156 NEUROSURGEON'S CHRISTMAS TO REMEMBER

thinking it was my fault. Even now, I can't let my instincts dictate my actions."

They sat there in silence for a while, staring out into the night, watching the snow gather on the windshield.

"We make quite a pair, don't we?" Max said at last, followed by a small, sad chuckle.

"Yeah, we do." She flipped on the wipers and the snow disappeared to reveal a Christmas tree lot across the parking area from them. Ayanna laughed. "Looks like the holidays are haunting you today."

Max grinned and shook his head. "It does, doesn't it? Maybe this is a sign I should give in to the spirit of Santa."

Ayanna looked over at him, her gaze narrowed. "Are you thinking what I'm thinking?"

"That we should decorate the suite so I can show you exactly what I mean about my superior Christmas tree composition theory?" Max gave a curt nod. "Yes. I say we do it. If you can squeeze it in around your work, that is."

She couldn't help smiling back. "With a challenge like that, how could I refuse?"

They got out and walked over to the brightly lit area. It was busy tonight, with several couples as well as a few families milling about to find "their" tree.

"How about these?" Ayanna said, appraising several small Douglas firs. "What do you think?"

Max checked them out then crossed his arms. "Too small. And the needles are dry. They'll all fall off before Christmas."

"Hmm." She bit back a grin. "Don't tell me your expertise extends to arborist as well."

"I just know my way around a spruce." He walked over to another specimen across the aisle, this one taller and plumper. "See, now this one is better. Lots of branches for ornaments, and the needles are strong and healthy. If you want a tree, this is the one to get. Should fit perfectly in that corner in the living room between the TV and the windows."

"You remind me of my dad. He used to give us lectures every year," Ayanna said, waving over one of the attendants so she could buy the tree Max had approved. "Drove my mom nuts. Him bossing her around with the lights and tinsel. Add in my brothers breaking every other ornament and my sisters fighting over who'd put the star on the top and that was pretty much every Christmas at Casa Franklin."

Max's smiled widened and Ayanna couldn't help grinning herself. So much so she didn't even notice the attendant behind her until she crashed into him. Flustered, she paid the guy then stood off to the side with Max while they ran the tree through the bundler to make it easier to load on top of the car with the bungee cords she kept in her trunk to hold cargo and boxes.

"I'll pay you for half the tree," Max said while they waited.

"Don't be ridiculous." Ayanna waved off his suggestion. "Consider this my thanks to you for helping me pick out the food for the ball. I seriously could not have gotten all that done without you."

"Fine. But since we stopped here, I insist we stop for food on the way back. And I will pay for it. We'll need fuel to get that thing decorated. Speaking of which, do we need to buy decorations too?"

"I actually have several boxes of them in storage while they're working on my apartment. We can pick them up after we get dinner." At his smug look she conceded, "What? All this activity has made me hungry."

"Whatever." Max held out his hand. "Deal?"

"Deal." They shook on it, the heat of him

warming her through her red knit mitten. The attendant finished bundling up their tree and they each grabbed a side to haul it back across the lot to the car. Max had just finished fastening the last bungee cord when a shout went out from the tree lot behind them.

"Help! Someone, please help me! My husband's collapsed!"

Max sprinted across the lot with Ayanna following close on his heels. They found an older woman kneeling on the ground beside a man who'd collapsed. Max knelt and checked for a heartbeat on the man's neck. "He's not breathing and his pulse is weak. Ayanna, call 911. Ma'am, I'm a doctor. Can you tell me if your husband has a heart condition?"

"Yes," the woman said, through her sobs. "He's got stents and is on blood thinners. Please help him. I don't know what I'd do if I lost him."

"I'll do everything I can, ma'am. Promise." Max positioned the man's head properly then puffed a breath into his patient's lungs before beginning compressions. "Ayanna, ETA on that ambulance, please?"

"911 Dispatch. What's your emergency?" the operator said over the line, and Ayanna's adrenaline skyrocketed.

"Yes, we're at the Christmas tree lot on

Holman Road, near Soundview Playfield, and there's a man who's collapsed. We think he might have had a heart attack. He's not breathing, and his pulse is weak. There's a doctor on scene, but we need an ambulance."

"I've got your coordinates on GPS, ma'am, and the EMTs are on the way. Please stay on the line with me until they arrive."

"I could use some help," Max said, looking up at Ayanna. "Do you know CPR?"

"I do." She'd had the mandatory training every year at her jobs, plus she had learned early on from her mother. Had never had to put it into practice, though, until tonight. She handed her phone to the man's wife. "Stay on the line with them until the ambulance arrives. I'm going to help the doctor with your husband."

The woman nodded, her hands shaking as she took the phone from Ayanna.

Ayanna was shaking pretty badly herself, but she needed to stay calm. Panic was your worst enemy in a crisis, her mom always said, and she would know. Not caring about the snowy wet pavement staining her designer pants, she knelt beside Max and helped get the man's coat and shirt open while Max pulled out his wallet to remove a face shield.

"Always carry one with me," he said at her questioning look. "Just in case."

Max repositioned the man's neck to open his airway again after placing the face shield then waited while Ayanna positioned her hands correctly on the guy's chest to begin compressions. "Ready?"

"Ready." Not really, but this was life or death. She nodded and Max puffed two breaths into the man's mouth before Ayanna started her compressions. To make sure she kept the correct rhythm and rate of one hundred to one hundred and twenty compressions per minute, she sang the Bee Gees song "Stayin' Alive" in her head.

"You're doing great," Max said, giving her an encouraging smile as the wail of a siren grew louder in the distance. "Let me know if you get tired and we can switch. Shouldn't be too long now."

"Yes," the man's wife said into Ayanna's phone. "They're doing CPR on him now. Please hurry!"

Time narrowed to just one second, then the next, as Ayanna helped Max try to save this man's life. He continued to check their patient's vitals and give breaths between her compressions. She had no idea how long they worked, but once the EMTs arrived and took over CPR from them, Ayanna's arms ached and her own chest felt tight from stress.

Max gave the medics a rundown on the man's condition then helped them load the man and his wife into the back of the waiting ambulance.

"Oh," the wife said, handing Ayanna back her phone. "Thank you both so much for all you've done."

Ayanna was still too stunned by everything that she couldn't do more than nod to the woman. Sirens wailed again as the ambulance took off, leaving her and Max standing in the parking lot while the gathered crowd around them dispersed. Several people shook her hand or clapped Max on the back as they left, congratulating them on a job well done.

She still couldn't wrap her head around what had happened. It seemed unreal. One minute they'd bought a tree, the next they were trying to save a life. As they walked back to the car again, her feet felt numb, not from cold but from shock.

"Maybe I should drive?" Max asked as she stopped in front of the SUV and just stood there. Ayanna didn't usually allow other people to take charge, but tonight it seemed like a good idea. She handed the keys to him.

"Right," he said, opening her door for her. "You'd better sit down before you fall down."

They got into her vehicle and she fumbled with her seatbelt, the distinctive scent from the tree strapped to the roof mixing with the antiseptic from the wipes the medics had used still swirling around her. Ayanna's fingers shook so badly Max ended up buckling her in. She felt shaken and stirred and yet oddly triumphant.

He started the engine, watching her. "You sure you're okay?"

"Yes. That was…" She had no words. "Wow."

"Let's just hope he'll survive and make a full recovery." He ran his hand through his hair again, melting snowflakes making the strands sparkle in the darkness. "Emergency situations like that are always tough, but you did well."

"So did you." Ayanna blinked at him. He'd done something miraculous and she was even more astonished by him than she'd been before. Every day since she'd known him, Max Granger had surprised her in the best possible ways. "You were amazing. Is your life that exciting every day?"

"Uh, no." His slow smile went a long way toward chasing away the chill that had settled in her bones during their ordeal. "And you were pretty spectacular yourself. Taking the classes for CPR and actually performing it in a crisis are two different things. Well done, Ayanna."

Heat crept up her cheeks and a bubble of joy swelled inside her. Before she could consider the wisdom of her actions, Ayanna leaned over and kissed him, soft and quick. When she pulled back, the air between them stilled and the world dropped away.

Say something.

Except when she opened her mouth, nothing came out.

Max looked as stunned as she felt, but recovered faster, facing front again and pulling out of the lot. "Right. Let's get your decorations and some food and get back to the suite before we get into more trouble."

Max's thoughts continued to whirl once they were back in the suite. At least wrestling the tree into position before the windows in the living room gave him some welcome space to breathe.

It wasn't the situation with the heart-attack victim the bothered him as he was used to dealing with emergencies in his line of work. What he wasn't used to dealing with were the emotions now roiling through him like a pot at full boil—need, nervousness, want, wariness. He'd kissed Ayanna Franklin twice and each time had left him questioning everything about himself and what he wanted.

He'd planned to stay alone, to keep his feelings safely tucked away where they couldn't hurt him. But one touch, one look, one valiant rescue effort on Ayanna's part had sent all his well-ordered, well-intentioned plans straight to hell.

She made him want to open up his heart and live and love again. And that was terrifying.

"Okay," Ayanna said, after she'd tightened the screws on the tree stand to lock their spruce into place. "Let's this gal beautified."

"Beautified?" Max squinted one eye. "Is that even a word?"

"It is in my family," she said, opening one of the boxes they'd retrieved from her storage pod. "Growing up, whenever I or my sisters went to get our hair done, my mom said we were getting beautified."

"Hmm." Max shrugged off his jacket and tossed it over the back of the sofa. "If we're going to decorate first, I'll put our food in the oven to keep it warm."

"Good idea." Ayanna set out ornaments

on the coffee table and sofa cushions, along with several strings of multi-colored lights. "Speaking of my mom, she really enjoyed having you there on Thanksgiving."

"I liked her too," he said as he stuck their bags of burgers and fries into the warming oven. "And I'm excited to try those recipes she gave me. She's an interesting lady."

"That's one way to put it." Ayanna chuckled and damn if he didn't feel that low, throaty sound straight in his groin. Man, he needed to get a grip on this thing between them before he did something stupid, like haul her into his arms and right into his bedroom. Thankfully, once he got back into the living room, Ayanna's mood seemed to have shifted from teasing to pensive. She continued while she set out more ornaments on the coffee table. "But you were right. I did learn to put other people's needs above my own when I was growing up. In some ways, I guess that's what makes me good at my job. I know what my clients want before they do sometimes."

Her self-reflection was good, even if it hurt his heart to see her smile disappear. Man, he loved that smile. "Anticipating others' needs isn't always a bad thing."

She gave a sad little snort. "True, but it

isn't always such a great trait in relationships. Especially when your partner uses it against you. When we first started dating, Will appreciated all the little things I did for him—making sure I kept his favorite tea in stock, arranging his calendar so he had time to hit the gym when he wanted, ordering supplies for his office so he never ran out.

"But then, after a few months, he came to expect it from me and if I got behind or forgot, he'd get angry. Then, finally, he turned it on me and began to tear me down for my caretaker tendencies, nitpicking at me about how he wished I wasn't such a control freak all the time and how I'd be so much more fun if I loosened up. Near the end, right before he ran off with Rinna, he told me I was lucky to have him because he put up with all my issues. He said another man wouldn't even consider getting involved with me."

She exhaled slowly and set the empty ornament container aside before picking up a ball of tangled lights from the sofa. "After the breakup and the wedding that wasn't, I didn't know what to think."

A small muscle spasmed near Max's tight jaw. The more she talked about her selfish ass of an ex, the more he wanted to punch the guy in the face. Ayanna was wonderful and witty and way too caring about everyone else's comfort but her own. If this Will guy couldn't see that, then he hadn't deserved her. Max went back to the kitchen for a pitcher of water to pour into the tree stand before they started decorating, talking to Ayanna over his shoulder as he went. "Please, tell me you didn't believe those awful things he said."

"I wish I could, at least at first, but honestly, I was too close to the situation." She shook her head. "My family had tried to warn me about him, especially my mom, but I blew her off. Said she was being too overprotective. I even accused her of being jealous because I was doing for Will what I'd always done for the family—taking care of him like I used to take care of them."

Max returned with the water, the plastic handle of the water pitcher clenched tightly in his fist to stop himself from reaching over and pulling Ayanna into his arms instead.

"Just one more way I was completely blind to what was really going on. God, I'm such an idiot. That night I walked in on him and Rinna in our bed…" She swallowed hard, her brows drawing together and her lips tightening. "Anyway, now, in hindsight, I can see that it was Will and not me who caused the breakup, but still. I have a hard time trusting my instincts. Back then, I thought I was helping, thought I was making things better, but I wasn't. It makes it difficult to open up again, you know?"

"I do." Max poured the water around the base of the tree then set the empty pitcher aside before grabbing a non-tangled string of lights to weave through the tree branches. "With the way I was raised, my parents being so cold and clinical around me, meeting Laura was a shock to my system. She was so different, like a bright light after years of darkness. But she was so easy to be around, so kind and caring, she made it easy for me to open up around her." He scowled as he disappeared around the back of the tree, then glanced over again at Ayanna when he emerged on the other side. "And it made it so much harder when she died. Sometimes I wonder if it would've been better not to have met her at all."

Ayanna stopped fiddling with the lights and gave him an astonished look. "You can't mean that. From what you've told me, you loved her a great deal. What's that saying? 'It's better to have loved and lost than never to have loved at all'?"

"I hate that saying." He cringed and gave a full-body shake then finished placing the last of his string of lights before walking over to grab another. "Up until I'd met her, I'd learned to live my life alone. Logically. Analytically. I was happy that way. After being married to Laura and seeing a different way, making myself open and vulnerable to that and then losing her, it was…" He searched for the right word. *Unnerving? Eviscerating? Excruciating?* Finally, he settled on, "The most difficult thing I've ever been through."

"I can't imagine," Ayanna said, frowning down at the knotted lights in her hands. "I mean, having Will run away with my ex-best friend right before our wedding was bad, and there are still days I wish karma would hurry up and do her thing where he's concerned, but death?" She sighed. "You mentioned in the car the other day that you felt responsible for what happened to your wife. I hope you know that Laura's passing wasn't your fault either."

Max compressed his lips. "I'm a doctor. I should have known."

"Exactly. You're a doctor, not a psychic." She laid her string of lights on the coffee table and fixed him with a steady stare. "Is what happened with her why you don't celebrate the holidays now?"

He turned away to tuck more lights into

the upper sections of the tree. "Partly, I suppose."

"Tell me more about her. What was she like? You said she was kind and caring."

"She was. Basically, the opposite of me," Max said, trying to ease the seriousness in the room with humor and failing, if the look Ayanna gave him was any indication. Finally, he gave in and sighed. "Fine. Let's see. We got married six months after we met. I knew right away she was the one. Laura used to tease me that it took her a lot longer." He chuckled, the old sting of guilt in his chest whenever he thought of his late wife easing slightly the more he talked to Ayanna.

"We bought a little house in Jericho, Long Island, since we both worked in Manhattan, and we started a life together." He pictured their little white two-story Tudor-style house. "We were happy there." Rather than rehash his painful past again, he changed course. "Laura loved Christmas. Loved all the holidays, really. If there was a reason to decorate and buy candy, she was on it."

"She sounds like my kind of lady." Ayanna grinned. "Cookies too. Don't forget the cookies."

"Never." A slow smile formed on his lips.

"By the way, I've got a recipe to try out later. Don't let me forget."

She tapped her temple. "Got it in my internal calendar."

"Good." He grabbed the string of lights she'd been working on off the table and tugged them free himself, the words flowing out now before he could stop them. Max didn't stop to consider why talking to Ayanna seemed so easy, just enjoyed the rare and delightful fact that it was. "Before Laura, I wasn't used to being a priority in someone's life. I got so used to being alone when I was a kid, I figured that's the way it would always be. That life was meant to be lived alone, that emotions were bad. But when I was with my wife, she made it okay to open up, to be vulnerable. Then that safety net disappeared."

He stuck the remaining lights on the upper branches of the trees then lowered his arms. "After she was gone, I closed myself off again, tried to lose myself in my work. I wanted that to be enough. I wanted to not feel anymore."

"Oh, Max." Ayanna moved in beside him, her lovely dark eyes filled with concern. "I'm so sorry."

"It's okay." He placed the last of the lights, then reached for one of her garlands. "But being at your parents' house on Thanksgiving was nice. Reminded me that things could be different, brighter."

Man, he'd not intended to share all this with her, but now that it was out there, he was glad. "How about we finish decorating later? I'm starving."

Ayanna watched him a moment, then nodded. "Okay, but first I'm going to change. Be right back."

Max gathered their dinner then sat at the dining table to wait, his thoughts ticking through the event of the night and wondering how exactly he was going to handle things with Ayanna from now on. Even with all they'd shared tonight, there were still secrets between them. Like how he was starting to care for her more than as just a friend. How he felt more connected to her every day. Most of all, how much he'd miss her after he left Seattle.

CHAPTER TEN

THE REST OF the week passed by in a blur of phone calls and appointments for Ayanna. Between hiring the small orchestra for the ball and finalizing the menus at the hotel, she'd been up to her eyeballs in work. Max had continued to help, though, and they both had the entire weekend ahead off, so she was looking forward to relaxing in the suite.

She glanced at him over the top of her book and bit back a smile. The man took his decorating seriously, that was for sure. He hadn't been kidding about his theory of composition thing either, considering it had taken him days to perfect the tree and he'd been standing there at least five minutes staring at one spot or another to decide where to hang the last ornament. Must be a surgeon thing, she figured.

Finally, he chose a branch and carefully

looped the tiny string around the needles then stood back.

"There. Done!"

Ayanna set her book aside and stood, her arm brushing his as she moved in beside him. She ignored the tingle of heat skittering across her skin from the brief contact and focused on his masterpiece instead. "Looks great."

He grinned down at her and damn if her insides didn't melt into a puddle of goo. "Thanks. Hey, what are your plans this afternoon?"

"Nothing, really." She blinked up at him, far too comfy in her cozy sweats to want to change. "Just stay here and read. Why?"

"Well…" He reached over to grab the newspaper off the coffee table. "I saw in here there's a Christmas parade downtown today. I've never been to one and thought maybe we could go."

Surprised, she blinked at him. "You. The former Grinch. Want to go to a Christmas parade?"

He shrugged and flashed her a crooked little half-smile, the one that made her heart dance a besotted jig. Lord, the man was adorable, and he wasn't even trying. She was in major trouble here.

"C'mon," he said, his tone turning pleading. "Just to see what it is, that's all. We have to go out anyway to get a couple of missing ingredients for my cookie recipe that I forgot to add to the grocery list the other day, and from the map on my phone it looks like the parade route is close by the store, so…" He flipped through more pages to the entertainment section. "Oh, and there's also a showing of *It's a Wonderful Life* across the street in Myrtle Edwards Park after the parade."

She checked the area behind him then glanced around the room.

"What are you doing?" Max frowned.

"Searching for the real Max Granger?"

"Funny. Not." He gave her a deadpan look. "I figured since we both had the weekend off, maybe you could show me around more of Seattle. I don't usually get the chance to sightsee when I'm traveling, and I like this city. Not my fault if it happens to be the holidays too." Max shrugged. "I mean, if you don't want to, that's fine. I can go by myself."

She probably should say no. Ayanna was getting far too attached to him already. But she couldn't bring herself to do it. Her book was good, but reality was even better today. "Fine. I'll go. I think they offer picnic meals at those movies too, if I'm not mistaken.

James and his partner David go to them a lot and said they're a lot of fun. They have them year round, since the winters are generally mild here in the PNW."

"Pacific Northwest," he said, with pride. "See? I'm even getting the lingo."

"You are." She winked then headed around the couch toward the hall. "Let me put my jeans on. Be right back."

"No rush. The parade doesn't start for another hour, so you've got time." He headed for the kitchen. "I'll clean up from breakfast while you get ready."

He'd made them yummy waffles with strawberries, whipped cream and thick-cut bacon and Ayanna thought she'd died and gone to heaven. The man had a way with food, no doubt about it. Had a way with people too, especially her. Yep. She had it bad for her brooding surgeon and that wasn't good.

Flustered and frustrated, in more ways than one, Ayanna changed into a fresh pair of jeans and a festive emerald-green turtleneck then headed into her bathroom to fix her hair and apply a light coat of makeup before going back out to find Max. He was just finishing up with the dishes and had put on a black sweater over his gray henley and faded jeans, she noticed.

He straightened after closing the dishwasher and caught sight of her, giving her a slow once-over that had her heart tripping. "You look… *Wow*. Green is definitely your color."

"Thanks." She ran a self-conscious hand down the front of her turtleneck. "You look nice too."

The black sweater clung to his torso in all the right spots and made her fingertips itch to slide beneath it to stroke his warm, soft skin. She tugged on her jacket and to keep from reaching for him instead.

"Should we go?" She slung her purse over her shoulder then turned fast, only to freeze in place as Max came over to slide his hands beneath the collar of her brown leather bomber jacket to free her curls trapped there. Ayanna's breath caught and her lips parted. If she rose up on tiptoe, she could kiss him. They could forget about the parade and the movie and stay in bed all day and…

Max's eyes flickered to her mouth then back to her eyes, the flames banked there matching her own. Then he took a deep breath and stepped back. "Ready?"

"Ready."

For more than you know.

She followed him out the door, excitement buzzing in her bloodstream.

"This is great," Max said later as they stood near the curb on Fourth Avenue and watched another high school marching band go by, this one playing the theme from *Home Alone*. "Not sure about the moose, though."

"You mean Mariner Moose and the Moose-mobile?" Ayanna laughed. "They're a Seattle tradition!"

"Right. Sure." He chuckled, then put his arm around her shoulders to keep them from getting separated in the crowds. Or at least that was the excuse he was going with anyway. Honestly, it felt so damned good to touch her he couldn't seem to stop. "Looks like the big guy in red is coming."

"Yes!" Ayanna clapped and pointed, excited as any of the kids nearby. It was great to see her enjoy herself. She worked too hard and he was determined to see her take better care of herself. Soon the booming strains of "Santa Claus is Coming to Town" filled the air and he pulled Ayanna closer as they waved to St. Nick and caught a few candy canes tossed by the elves on board the sleigh. Finally, she turned to him, her smile glowing brighter than the lights decorating the storefront windows. "That was awesome! I haven't been to one of these since I was a kid. Thanks for bringing me."

"Thanks for coming." Without thinking, he looped his other arm around her waist and clasped his hands at the small of her back. "Ready to see the movie now?"

"Absolutely. Lead the way!" She hugged him then took his hand as they walked down the street and over to the park. They picked up a free blanket at a concession stand nearby then spread it out on the grass beneath a tree, so they'd have something to rest back on. A vendor came around with sandwiches and chips and Max bought them each a sack lunch and a bottled water to enjoy. The park filled up quickly with couples and he couldn't remember the last time he'd sat outside like this and relaxed. In the distance, boats filled Puget Sound for a nautical holiday celebration and the low toots of their horns reminded him that they were still on the coast and not lost at the North Pole.

Being here with Ayanna, happiness coursing through his veins, made him reconsider. Maybe there was something to be said for the holidays after all. For the first time in a long time Max realized he didn't dread Christmas. And it was all thanks to the woman beside him.

For the next few hours, they sat side by side, his arm around Ayanna and her head on his shoulder, chatting and eating and watching Jimmy Stewart and Clarence, his guardian angel, come to the conclusion that as hard as things had been in the past, there'd been good times too. Everything had led them to that point in time. One difference and it would all change.

The irony wasn't lost on Max.

After the final scene of Jimmy and his on-screen family standing in a snowy Bedford Falls, staring up at the starry sky as Clarence got his wings, Ayanna gave a happy sigh and swiped the back of her hand across her damp cheeks. "Man, no matter how many times I see that movie, it always gets me. How about you, Grinch? Did you like it?"

"Seriously? That's your nickname for me?" He laughed and squeezed her closer into his side for a minute. "Fine. I can live with it. And, yes, I liked it." He'd seen it before. Who hadn't? But today, for some reason, its message really hit home. After letting her go and clambering to his feet, Max helped Ayanna up then turned to throw away their trash while she folded up their blanket to return it to the concession booth. "My favorite old holiday movie, though, is *The Bishop's Wife*, with Cary Grant."

"Oh, that's a good one too." She walked alongside him back toward the street "Anything with Cary Grant is great, really. Where to now?"

"Now we stop at the grocery store so I can pick up a few last things to make my special cookies." He took her hand as they crossed the street. Today they weren't busy professionals with stressful jobs and people depending on them. They were just two people out for a day of fun and holiday cheer. It felt good. And right.

They got his supplies then returned to the hotel. Once he'd removed his coat and helped Ayanna with hers, he checked his phone while Ayanna got out mixing bowls and set the oven to preheat to the temperature he'd given her. After dialing the number for the nurses' station in ICU, Max turned away to make his call.

The ICU charge nurse picked up on the second ring. "Intensive Care, Laurel speaking."

"Hi, Laurel. Dr. Granger checking in on the condition of my patient, please." He paced the small area while he waited for the nurse to pull up the King's file on the computer. After a busy day, Max usually felt drained. But now he was restless with energy. He found it harder to resist the pull he felt toward Ayanna. If he'd been looking, she was everything he wanted—smart, funny, outgoing, caring, loyal. But he wasn't looking.

Am I?

"Yes, Dr. Granger," Laurel said, bringing him back to reality. "The King's condition is still stable. His GCS is holding steady at six and he's breathing well with the ventilator."

"Okay." The fact that some weeks had passed and the King still hadn't regained consciousness yet wasn't ideal, but they had him under constant monitoring and his latest CT scans hadn't shown any new bleeding or clot formation, so that was promising. Plus, the King's son, Dr. di Rossi, had spent a lot of his time at his father's bedside, speaking to him and holding his hands. Research showed such actions helped many coma patients recover more quickly and several articles cited how coma patients could still hear things being said to and around them. Max was a firm believer in the power and support of community to help heal patients' wounds and new theories about the mind-body-immune-system connection arose each day. "Good. Continue the current protocol then. And be sure to call me right away if anything changes."

"Will do, Doctor," Laurel said, and ended the call.

Max then spoke with Dr. di Rossi about his father's condition before putting his phone on the charging pad. Time to bake. With Ayanna. The thought thrilled him more than he'd expected.

"So, where's the recipe?" Ayanna had taken off her shoes, he noticed, leaving her in stockinged feet. A sudden urge to make her cute little toes curl with ecstasy had his throat constricting with need again before he swallowed hard.

"Uh." Max turned his attention to measuring out ingredients to distract himself. "It's in my head."

"You sound like my mom. She's got her favorites memorized too. I'm actually surprised she wrote them down for you. She must like you, since she doesn't do that for just anyone." She moved in beside him at the island, her warmth sending a fresh wave of want through him. His hands shook slightly as he cracked eggs into the bowl. Lord, the woman affected him in the best, and worst, way. Ayanna threw away the empty eggshells then washed her hands. "What can I do?"

"Give me a minute to get all this mixed together," he said, reaching into the fridge for the milk and butter and a bag of crushed pecans, grateful for the blast of chilly air on his overheated body. "Then you can help me get the dough on those cookies sheets. Go ahead and line them with parchment paper, if you want."

"Will do."

Once ready, they each took a tablespoon and scooped out small balls of dough, rolling them into one-inch spheres and coating each in crushed pecans before placing them on the cookie sheets. Max glanced over at her batch of twelve. "Good. Now go down each row and stick your thumb into the center of each ball."

She did, licking her thumb after she'd finished. And damn if Max couldn't stop thinking about where else he'd like her to use that soft pink tongue of hers now. Heat prickled up his neck from beneath the collar of his sweater and he wondered when the heck it had gotten so hot in the suite. He quickly shoved the cookie sheets into the oven and set the timer.

"Now we wait eight minutes until they're done then do it all again." He turned away to wash his hands, his body screaming for him to forget about his good intentions and just take Ayanna to bed. But his analytical mind still urged caution. This wouldn't be another emotionless one-night stand. He cared for Ayanna, more than he'd been willing to admit until now, and he wasn't used to all these feelings roiling around inside him.

It was exhilarating. It was exhausting. It was unlike anything he'd ever experienced.

He dried his hands then fiddled with the towel, avoiding facing Ayanna again until he was certain he had himself back under control.

"So," she said behind him, her tone quiet. "What do you call these cookies?"

Right. The cookies. Their sweet, familiar scent wafted from the oven as they baked. He reached back into the fridge to pull out a jar of currant jelly. "Thumbprint Cookies."

"Imagine that." Ayanna snorted and took the jar from him. "And what's this for?"

"To put a dollop in the center of each cookie after they've cooled." He twisted off the lid then got out two clean teaspoons. "You can help me fill them, if you want."

"Absolutely."

The buzzer went off a short time later and he pulled the pans out of the oven with an oven mitt, setting them atop the stove to cool before removing the baked cookies and freeing up the pans for another round. They worked side by side, making a surprisingly good team. So good, in fact, Max couldn't help thinking about where else they might make fine partners. He shook his head and cracked a joke to distract himself from the tsunami of desire threatening to pull him under. "I think you're eating more dough than you're putting on the cookie sheets."

"Maybe." She laughed. "But these are so good. Seriously. You should enter them in the staff cookie contest tomorrow."

Max scrunched his nose. "I'm not really part of the staff."

"You are for now. It'll be fun. And maybe you'll even win."

He sighed and tried to bite back the grin threatening to break through his stoic façade. "What's the prize?"

"Besides bragging rights? Michelin-starred dinner for two." She shoved another bite of dough in her mouth then winked. "For a foodie like you, that's like nirvana, right?"

Hell, yeah, he wanted to win that prize. "Consider me convinced."

"Cool!" Ayanna fisted pumped the air. "I'm getting you out of your shell at last."

"Are you always like this?" he teased, already knowing the answer.

"Only when it's something important to me," she said, their gazes catching and holding before they both looked away. He'd not missed the flicker of heat in her dark eyes or the answering flare of need in his gut. They each retreated to their own corners of the kitchen, the air between them sparking like a live wire.

Finally, after what seemed a small eternity, all the cookies were done, half of them filled with currant jelly, and the oven was off. The suite smelled like the holidays and Max still had no idea what to do about this thing between him and Ayanna. She was still beside him, spooning jelly into their cookies and occasionally licking the sugar off her fingers. Each time he watched her suck on a fingertip, he moved that much closer to moaning, his body taut with need. She was going to kill him if this didn't stop soon. Death by desire.

"There," she said, filling the last cookie. "All done. What do you think?"

I think I'd like to spread that jelly on you next and lick it off every square inch of you.

Max cleared his throat. "I think that's enough baking for now."

He turned away to fill the sink with soapy water, then shoved the cookie sheets and utensils in to soak. "Thanks for your help."

"Thanks for letting me." Ayanna leaned her hip against the counter beside him and crossed her arms. "And thanks for today too. I think you might have even enjoyed yourself."

"I did." He shut off the faucet and swiped a hand through his hair. "It was fun."

"Oh." She bit her lips, stifling a laugh. "You've got suds on your forehead."

Ayanna brushed her finger across his skin to remove the soap and his mouth dried to sandpaper. Oh, God. Every cell in his body raged to have her. Teeth clenched, he forced himself not pick her up and take her right there on the counter. He might've kept his control too, if her touch hadn't traveled down his cheek then around to the nape of his neck, ruffling his hair and making him shiver.

Yep. Every man had his limits and Max Granger had just reached his.

Before he could second-guess his actions, he tugged Ayanna against him, kissing her hard and hot and deep. His free hand slid down to pull her hips against his, letting her feel just how much he wanted her. Instead of objecting to his advances, Ayanna couldn't seem to get enough, sliding her fingers into his hair and holding him tighter, her legs wrapping around his waist. He hoisted her up and instead of taking her in the kitchen he headed for the master bedroom, not wanting to rush their first time together.

Max set her in the middle of his huge king-sized bed and tore off his sweater and T-shirt before joining Ayanna. Her clothes and his jeans and boxer briefs vanished in a tangle of kisses and caresses and soon they were both naked atop the down-filled comforter. She felt every bit as amazing against him as he'd imagined, and Max took his time exploring her beautiful body. Worshiped her gorgeous breasts, then kissed his way down her body to make love to her with his mouth and tongue, showing her how much he cared, all the things he couldn't say.

Ayanna moaned and writhed beneath him, crying out her pleasure as the soft glow of twinkle lights filtered in from the tree in the living room.

Once she'd settled back to earth, Max slowly kissed his way back up to her lips, loving the dreamy look in her lovely eyes. Loving even more that he'd been the one to put it there. He rested his forehead against hers, his breathing heavy and his body tense, needing release of its own. "Hang on."

He fumbled in the nightstand drawer for the complimentary condom packets he'd found in there on his first night. Originally, he'd thought them a frivolous amenity. Now he couldn't be happier this five-star hotel had thought of everything. While he put it on, Ayanna raised up on her elbows to watch. Knowing she wanted him every bit as much as he wanted her only made the whole thing hotter. Still, he wanted to be sure before they took the final step. There was no going back after this.

"Are you sure?" He held himself above her with one forearm, his hard length poised at her wet entrance. "I need to know—"

Ayanna growled and pulled him down for another kiss. "Get inside me, Max. Now."

She didn't have to ask twice. He drove into her in one long thrust then held still to allow her body to adjust to his size. Then she dug her heels into his backside and rocked her hips and he set up a rhythm that had them both teetering on the edge of ecstasy. He couldn't stop kissing her. Her mouth. Her cheeks. Her throat. Her breasts. Ayanna met him thrust for thrust, those long, manicured nails of hers scoring his back and bringing him closer and closer to orgasm.

At first he'd been worried about it not being good between them. But now he worried he might never find another person who matched him so perfectly. She seemed to know, instinctively, exactly what he wanted, how to move to draw every single last shred of feeling from him. Ayanna cried out again and he reached between them to stroke her most sensitive flesh. That was all it took. She arched hard, reaching her second climax and spurring him on to his own fulfillment. He thrust once, twice, then went whipcord tight as wave after wave of pleasure drowned him in an explosion of sensation.

Afterward, they lay sated in each other's arms, Ayanna stroking her fingers through his hair while he dozed with his head on her breast, the steady beat of her heart lulling him into blissful sleep.

CHAPTER ELEVEN

AYANNA WOKE EARLY the next morning and stared around the unfamiliar bedroom, taking a moment to register where she was. Max's bedroom. They'd made love. Several times. The warm weight of his arm wrapped around her waist as he spooned her from behind, his soft snores stirring the hair near her temple. Slowly, she turned over to face him, taking in his relaxed features, so unguarded in sleep.

Last night had been wonderful. Magical. And more than a tad scary.

The most terrifying part was that she hadn't felt this way about anyone since Will. She liked Max. Liked talking to him, liked spending time with him. Liked everything about him, way, way more than she should. Unable to resist, she gently smoothed an errant lock of hair off his forehead, the same one that had started it all in the kitchen last night.

Man, she'd never intended to fall for anyone again, let alone Max Granger, yet here she was, head over heels for him. Her heart felt ten sizes too big for her chest and all she wanted to do was stay in their warm bed, in his warm arms, for the rest of the day.

Except the longer she lay there, the more her old doubt demons kicked in, warning her about how quickly everything had become real between her and Max. Maybe too quickly. Her chest tightened and her throat constricted. Was she wrong again? Could she trust her feelings this time? What if her instincts were leading her astray, the same way they had before, blinding her to what was really happening?

Anxiety rushed through her and she suddenly couldn't stay there any longer. She needed to move, to breathe, to take some time alone to figure all this out. Originally, they'd both had the full weekend off, but after last night…

Nope. She eased out from under Max's arm. Besides, after spending yesterday with Max in a veritable winter wonderland, she had all sorts of new ideas for the centerpieces for the ball tables and décor for the ballroom and she really ought to get them nailed down before she forgot. Time was of the essence now with the big fundraiser in just a few days. She didn't want to lose that creative momentum when Dr. di Rossi and the entire Seattle General board of directors were depending on her.

At least, that's the excuse she was going with.

Ayanna gathered her clothes then headed into her own room to get dressed. After showering and changing, she padded to the kitchen, shoes in hand to keep from making too much noise, and brewed some coffee. Drank a cup of liquid energy while staring at the plate of cookies from the night before, remembering how much fun they'd had making them. She hadn't been kidding about him entering them in the cookie contest today and packed up a plateful to take with her.

Once she'd finished her coffee and eaten an extra cookie or three, Ayanna grabbed her coat and bag and the container full of cookies for the contest, then scribbled a quick note for Max before heading out to Seattle General.

Went in to work for a bit. See you later. And don't worry. I've got your cookies.

* * *

The annoying hotel alarm clock on the nightstand buzzed Max awake. He fumbled an arm over to shut it off without opening his eyes then he reached beside him to pull Ayanna closer, only to encounter cold mattress.

Frowning, he squinted over to confirm, yep. She was gone.

Damn. He'd envisioned them staying in bed together all day long.

Disappointed, Max rolled over onto his back and stared up at the white ceiling, listening for sounds of her in the suite, thinking maybe it wasn't too late to convince her to stay beneath the covers with him. But nope. Everything was quiet, indicating she'd already left the suite. With a groan, he got up, hitting the bathroom to take a quick shower then dressing in comfy sweats instead of his usual work clothes. Last night had been… *wonderful*.

Ayanna was beautiful and sexy. Yes, they'd only known each other a short time, but when you clicked with someone, you just clicked. It had been that way with Laura too. They'd only dated a few months before he'd asked her to marry him.

That thought tripped him up a minute. He liked Ayanna. More than liked her. But was he thinking of more with her? Was he considering forever?

Am I?

Deep in thought, he went out to the kitchen to make himself some tea. Being with Ayanna was great. Even spending the day at her parents' house on Thanksgiving had been nice. Meeting her siblings, enjoying that easy camaraderie of people who knew everything about you—good and bad—and loved you anyway. That had been a concept he'd never known he needed in his life until that day.

But old habits died hard and his analytical mind refused to stop turning things over in his head. As a brain surgeon, Max relied on being able to see and approach his cases from all angles to choose the best direction for treatment. But when it came to romance, nothing was ever that clear or concise. Love was messy and mind-boggling at times. Exactly why he tended to avoid it.

But somehow, with Ayanna, maybe the prospect wouldn't be so daunting.

After filling the kettle and setting it on the stove to boil, Max spotted the note Ayanna had left him.

Went in to work for a bit. See you later. And don't worry. I've got your cookies.

He chuckled and set the note aside, catching a hint of her spicy sweet perfume on the paper. Who knew, maybe she was right. Maybe his recipe would win that contest and they'd dine at a gorgeous seaside gourmet restaurant overlooking Puget Sound before he left to return to Manhattan.

The reminder of life in New York put a bit of a damper on his good mood. He was comfortable here with Ayanna. He didn't want to think about leaving yet. He shook his head and scolded himself. Forget about romance. The real reason he was here was the King's surgery. He had a job to do and a patient to monitor. And if the King's condition continued to improve, he could perform surgery as scheduled. That's where his focus should be. Everything else was irrelevant, no matter how his chest might ache whenever he thought of saying goodbye to Ayanna.

He finished his tea and made himself a quick egg white omelet before deciding to head into the hospital himself. Sitting around the empty suite wasn't his idea of a fun day and, besides, he had work and consults to keep him busy. The weather looked decent too, so the walk would do him good. Seattle General was only a few blocks away after all.

* * *

Half an hour later, the brisk morning air slapped his cheeks as he walked out of the hotel and headed east. The skies were overcast as usual, but the temp seemed less chilly. As he passed the storefronts filled with holiday cheer, he wondered about the man they'd saved at the tree lot and made a note to check on his condition when he got to work. More memories filtered into his head as he waited at the corner for the light to change. The way Ayanna had felt last night—against him, beneath him, around him. The soft moan of his name on her lips as she'd come apart in his arms. The sweet taste of her kisses, sugar and a bit of tartness from the currant jelly.

The light turned green and he crossed with a small crowd headed in the same direction. Even this early in the day, the tourists were out, dressed in red and green for the upcoming holiday, laden with shopping bags from the stores downtown. He reached Seattle General and headed straight to the emergency department to change into some scrubs in the staff locker room. From there he went up to ICU to see King Roberto. His last text update from a few hours prior suggested his patient's condition was still unchanged. That was good, considering the King's advanced age and what he'd been through during that accident.

He took the elevator up to the third floor and stepped off into the quiet environment, the rhythmic beeps of monitors and the occasional squeak of the staff's shoes on the gleaming linoleum the only sounds breaking the silence. The scents of antiseptic and lemon floor wax helped center him and focus him on the task at hand as he made his way to the nurses' station.

"Dr. Granger checking in," he said to the middle-aged woman behind the desk. "Any changes with my patient?"

"Still the same, Doc," the nurse said, grinning at him. "Congrats, by the way."

Max frowned. "For what?"

"Those are some fine cookies you entered in the contest, Doc Granger," Laurel said, coming up beside him. "What do we have to do to get the recipe?"

"Uh…" Totally confused, Max frowned at the assembled nurses around him. "You mean I won?"

"You did," the nurse behind the desk said. Her name tag said "Rosie." "Congrats."

"Wow." Max raised his eyebrows. "I didn't expect that."

"So, about that recipe, Doc," Laurel said,

her dark skin contrasting with her pink scrub shirt.

"Uh, sure." Max grabbed a piece of copy paper and pen and scribbled it down for them. "Here you guys go."

"Thanks, Doc," Laurel said, taking the paper over to the copy machine. "I'll try it out on my kids this year and see what they think. Enjoy that dinner too."

"Thanks, ladies," he said, heading for the King's room. He'd have to stop by Ayanna's office when he was done and thank her for entering him in the contest. She'd been right. Dinner at a five-star restaurant, just the two of them, was exactly his idea of nirvana.

CHAPTER TWELVE

ON THE NIGHT OF the fundraising ball, Ayanna honestly didn't know if she was coming or going, she was so busy. And nervous. Her caretaker instincts were out of control too, making her run from one corner of the massive ballroom to the other, checking on food and drinks and musicians and décor and any other issues that came up throughout the evening. Not to mention the running was made harder by the form-fitting emerald-green evening gown and silver strappy heels she'd worn for the event.

With a sigh, she stopped near the open bar and surveyed the space. The guests seemed happy. That was the most important thing. Happy donors meant larger donations and tonight was all about raising funds to add a new children's cancer ward at Seattle General. She smoothed a hand down the silky fabric of her dress and scanned the gathering crowd around her for Max.

"Stop worrying," he'd said, kissing her before they'd parted in the suite. "You look amazing and the ball will be amazing too. Enjoy the benefits of all your hard work!"

Except that was easier said than done for Ayanna. Max had been right again. She was used to constantly taking care of everyone else's problems, not relaxing and enjoying herself. They were arriving separately tonight, as she'd been here early to supervise her staff and make sure everything was set up properly ahead of the guests' arrivals. Now, though, she wished he'd come with her. Having Max by her side steadied her, grounded her. And, darn it, she missed him, even though it had only been a few hours since they'd parted.

Other than their working hours, they'd been practically inseparable since the night they'd made love. He'd even taken her for dinner last night. The food had been wonderful and the company even better. And the views from the floor-to-ceiling glass windows to the harbor below had been breathtaking. What she remembered most of all, though, was the warmth in Max's gray eyes and the touch of his skin on hers as he'd held her hand across the table. Things between them this week had been perfect.

Maybe too perfect.

Her heart lurched a bit before she shook it off. Her stupid instincts, mouthing off again. Max wasn't Will, she reminded herself. She could trust Max. And speaking of him, there he stood in the entrance, as if summoned from her thoughts. Her pulse stumbled and her knees went weak. Man, oh, man. Seeing her sexy surgeon in scrubs was a sight to behold. But Max dressed to the nines in a tuxedo? Be still, her racing heart. Talk about a glorious sight to behold. Their gazes caught across the crowded ballroom and held, and that's when she knew for certain.

I love Max Granger.

Totally. Completely. Irrevocably.

Oh, God.

Flustered, Ayanna forced her attention away from him and focused on the important guests milling about the ballroom beneath the beautiful gilded Aurora Dome. The elaborate, art-deco style stained-glass panels and intricate fresco work were illuminated tonight in shades of crimson and forest green for the occasion. On the tables were the elaborate centerpieces she'd chosen after seeing the Christmas parade floats with Max, made of white lilies and red roses. Even the glittering crystal glassware and sparkling silverware held a nineteen-twenties-style flavor. It all looked like a very expensive holiday heaven. Exactly what she was going for and, hopefully, exactly what would get their donors to open up their wallets to support the new children's cancer ward.

Dr. di Rossi and Dr. Featherstone, the King's orthopedic surgeon, stood not far away, and Ayanna made her way over to them, eager for something to distract her from Max and her newly acknowledged feelings for him. Along the way, she stopped to greet their high-profile attendees, everyone from celebrities to politicians to sports stars, using her formidable memory to place names with faces and make everyone feel welcome. Finally, she reached Dr. di Rossi and Dr. Featherstone as they sipped champagne taken from the tray of a passing server. When she didn't immediately say anything Dr. di Rossi quirked one eyebrow in question.

"Sorry... I was just wondering if you liked that risotto ball."

"It was delicious."

"And have you tried the smoked salmon? Or the chicken satay skewers?"

"I've tried the chicken skewers," Dr. Featherstone said. 'They're delicious, too." She looked beautiful in a crimson gown with lace straps and a full skirt of silk cascading from her hips. The color suited the woman's complexion perfectly and if the covert glances Dr. di Rossi kept giving Dr. Featherstone beneath his lashes were any indication, he seemed to agree.

"You've done a wonderful job of organizing this ball—I'm so impressed."

"Me too," Dr. di Rossi said, turning his head to look over Ayanna's shoulder.

Ayanna followed his gaze and caught sight of Max again, heading in her direction now. *Oh, boy.* Her mouth dried and she looked away fast, heat rising in her cheeks. If she wasn't careful, everyone would know by the end of the night exactly how she felt about him, including the man himself, and she wasn't sure if she was ready for that yet.

Get a grip, girl. Stay cool.

Ayanna smoothed a hand down the front of her fitted emerald-green gown. She'd purchased it weeks ago, before she'd met Max. Now she was glad of the color, considering the compliment he'd give her the day of the parade. Thoughts of that day quickly gave way to that night, Max naked and flushed as he'd driven them both to the peak of pleasure and...

Cheeks hot, she looked up to find Dr. Featherstone watching her and Ayanna fumbled to pick up the thread of conversation. Even though she couldn't see him behind her, her skin tingled with anticipation as Max grew closer to them by the second. Was it weird she could sense his presence? She'd never had that happen before and it seemed odd.

Focus, girl. Focus.

Max was right behind her now, his warmth fizzing through her like the bubbles in the expensive champagne in her glass and his scent—sandalwood and cedar and soap—made her want to close her eyes and just inhale his essence. He placed his hand at the small of her back and her pedicured toes curled in her expensive designer sandals.

Get. A. Grip. This is your big night. Don't blow it.

Determined to regain control, Ayanna squared her shoulders and stiffened her spine, causing Max's hand to fall away. It was difficult enough to think with him standing near her. With him touching her, her brain turned to mush.

"Hi, Max," Dr. di Rossi said. "We're just

saying what an amazing job Ayanna's done with the decorations and catering for tonight."

Max gave a polite nod to Dr. di Rossi and smiled at Ayanna. If they weren't careful everyone at Seattle General would know they were sleeping together and once the rumor mill got started who knew when it would die down? Gossip was a horrible thing. She knew that from experience. After the whole mess with Will, she'd spent months avoiding people's pitying looks and comments.

This isn't the same.

"Excuse me… I'd better go check on how things are going in the kitchen."

She'd almost reached the doorway when Max caught up to her and grabbed her hand.

"Dance with me," he said.

"I need to check on the food." Ayanna tried to pull away as he tugged her forward, but he held fast. "I've got a lot to do to make sure the guests are happy."

"What about you?" he asked, pulling her into his arms and swaying with her in time to the music, his embrace quieting the stress inside her. "Are you happy?"

Yes.

Instead of answering, she placed her hands

on his lapels and smoothed them down his chest.

"Everything is beautiful," Max said against her temple, his warm breath fanning her skin. "Including you."

"Thanks." She wanted to burrow into him and never leave, but that niggle of doubt persisted in the back of her mind. He'd never mentioned feeling the same way about her. Yes, they were happy now, but what if it all disappeared in an instant? That's what had happened with Will. She'd been blind to the truth. What if the same was happening now? Her emotions twisted and tangled, Ayanna forced herself to straighten and step back from him. "Sorry. But I'm working tonight and I really do need to check in on wait staff now. Excuse me."

Before he could stop her, she fled. Yes, she loved Max, but what if love wasn't enough? She took a deep breath then pushed through into the busy back area, the delicious smells of roasting meat and spices surrounding her. Todd and a couple of other members of her staff were already there, overseeing things. She checked in with them then inspected the cakes the bakery had delivered. They all looked perfect, from the smooth fondant frosting in graduated shades of grays and blacks on the London Fog cakes to the creamy white frosting of the vegan chocolate raspberry cake. Edible art, as Max had called them. She turned fast, only to run smack into the man himself, blocking her path.

"Mind telling me why you keep running away?" Max asked, not letting her get away again.

Ayanna opened her mouth then closed it again and Max shook his head. He'd not seen a takeoff that fast since the Indy 500. Something was going on and it was more than just nerves over her big night.

When she still didn't say anything after a few moments, he switched tactics. The last thing he wanted to do during the ball was argue with her. That wouldn't do either of them any good. Instead, he took her hand and gently let her back toward the exit. "Come on, we didn't finish our dance."

"But I need to—"

"No, you don't. Whatever it is, it can wait."

He took her out of the kitchen and onto the balcony just as the orchestra began one of his personal favorites: "Have Yourself A Merry Little Christmas." Its bittersweet lyrics always touched his heart, but now they seemed even more poignant because of the woman in his arms. He tucked her closer against him and her stiff posture relaxed at last, her body sinking into his and sending tingles of sweet awareness through him.

After years of struggle and strain, things were going well for him—with Ayanna and with his case. After his conversation with Dr. di Rossi he'd brought in Dr. Connor, one of the emergency room physicians who'd worked on the King and his family after the accident and a good friend of Dr. di Rossi's, as well and had told them both that as long as the King's condition continued to remain stable, they could proceed with the scheduled surgery on the fifteenth. Max had another CT scan scheduled for the King tomorrow morning and would know more after that. But for now his attention was completely on the woman in his arms. He couldn't resist sliding a hand down to Ayanna's lower back to pull her hips closer to his.

"Max." She pushed at his chest, forcing more space between them. "People will notice."

"So?" He looked down at her. "Who cares?"

"I care." She frowned, glancing through the French doors at the other couples dancing inside. "I have to work with these people."

"So do I," he said, looking down into her

beautiful brown eyes. "But how about we forget about that. Just for one night. You've put in hours and hours to get this ball ready. Now it's time to enjoy it."

Ayanna sighed and shook her head. "I know. You're right, and I'm sorry. It's just hard for me. I'm not used to letting go."

"I know." He smiled and rested his forehead against hers, glad she didn't push him away again. "Just know I'll be here to catch you. Don't worry. You can trust me."

"Can I?" she asked, the hesitation in her tone sending a surge of protectiveness through him.

"Yes, you can. I'm here for you, Ayanna. Whatever you need. You can rely on me."

She seemed to contemplate that for a moment, her brows drawing together, and he prayed his sincerity showed through in his voice. When she didn't respond, he exhaled and gazed up at the lighted dome visible inside the ballroom then back at her. "What's the dome called again?"

"The Northern Star."

Max smiled. "Then let me be that for you. Let me be your Northern Star, Ayanna."

She blinked up at him, the flash of hope in her dark eyes making his breath catch. Maybe he'd finally gotten through to her this time. Maybe she'd finally realize she could trust him, let him in, that he wasn't like her ex. Then her walls seemed to come down again, shutting him out. Snorting, Ayanna tried to pull away from him, using humor to keep him at bay. "Like my own personal GPS."

"I'm serious," he said, allowing her to move away from him when she stepped back.

"I know." A small sad smile formed on her lips. "But I'm not lost."

"Aren't you?" Max said, but doubted she'd heard him as she turned and disappeared into the throng of guests. Because he sure as hell felt like he was wandering in a forest of uncomfortable and unexpected feelings with no sense of how he'd ever find his way out again.

CHAPTER THIRTEEN

UNFORTUNATELY, THE KING'S CT scans the following morning did not look good.

In fact, based on the fact the images had shown that his meningioma had grown during the coma and now threatened to infiltrate the sagittal sinus, Max found himself scrubbing down and prepping for surgery to remove the King's tumor on the original date set for the King's operation—December fifteenth. Having blood flow compromised could have lethal consequences, so the procedure needed to happen before the tumor progressed any farther. Thankfully, he'd planned it all ahead of time using his model and other 3D programs on his computer so he was prepared. Dr. di Rossi hadn't been so fortunate, however, when Max had called to tell him the news earlier. Unfortunately, life wasn't always tidy.

The last thing Max wanted was to ignore

the warning signs and have disaster strike again.

The old pang of guilt he'd carried with him since his wife's death constricted his ribcage for the first time in weeks. Being with Ayanna had given him hope that he'd put that behind him for good, but it seemed the situation with the King had resurrected his old demons. They were another distraction he couldn't afford now, however, so Max pushed them aside. The long surgery ahead would be grueling enough.

Flipping the switch on his emotions, Max went into neurosurgeon mode and backed out of the prep room into the OR. The King was already on the table and ready to go. While the nurses gowned him up and tied on his mask, Max ran through the surgery in his mind, visualizing each step. Once he was suited up, Max approached the table and checked in with the anesthesiologist.

"Morning, Dr. Chen. Patient doing well?" Max asked. The King was lying face down on the surgical table with his head fixed in place to the right and a portion of his scalp shaved.

"Patient's stable and his vitals look good, Dr. Granger. Ready when you are," Dr. Chen said.

"Right. Let's get started."

* * *

Two hours into the four-hour procedure, Max was ready to begin the delicate process of removing the King's tumor, using ultrasonic aspiration.

"Fornices protected?" Max asked the assisting surgeon.

"Yes, Dr. Granger."

"Good. Thank you. Dr. Chen, how are the patient's vitals?"

"Still within normal limits. Blood pressure has dropped slightly, but O2 sat level is good."

"Okay. Proceeding with aspiration." Max held his instruments steady as he worked, occasionally asking for suction or irrigation but otherwise keeping silent. With the King's condition already compromised from the previous emergency craniotomy, he didn't want to take longer than necessary. Finally, an hour later, the tumor had been removed and the OR as a whole released a prolonged sigh of relief. The worst part was over. Now, Max just had to close and—

A shrill beep issued from the heart monitor and his attention snapped to the anesthesiologist. Sudden flashes of the day Laura had died flashed through Max's mind before he could stop them.

"There was nothing we could do."

Max swallowed hard and narrowed his gaze on the monitor. "What's happening, Dr. Chen?"

"Heart rate dropped." The anesthesiologist reached over to check the King's tracheal tube. "Breathing is normal."

"Have Cardiology on standby, please, just in case." Then the alarm stopped and the regular beeps of the King's pulse returned. Max flexed his tense fingers. "Zero-five suture, please."

A further hour and a half later, the King's surgery was over and the patient was on his way back to Radiology for a second MRI to make sure they'd removed the entire tumor. An odd mix of energy and exhaustion flooded Max's system, not uncommon after a complex surgery. Today, though, he also couldn't seem to stop thinking about Ayanna. Normally, he never let his personal life enter his mind during his operations, but now all that had changed.

"Dr. Granger?" One of the nurses waved him over to the computer monitor on the wall of the OR. "MRI results on the patient are in."

He removed his gloves then scrolled through

the images, happy to see they'd gotten all of the tumor and removed the risk. "These look good. Thank you, everyone. The patient is out of danger and should recover nicely."

Max went back into the prep room to remove his soiled gown and mask then washed up before exiting once more into the hallway. After updating Dr. di Rossi on his father's outcome and prognosis—both good—he headed back to his office to type up his report.

Once there, though, he found himself thinking even more about Ayanna. He'd checked her office, but her staff had said she was at a meeting. Now that the surgery was over, Max's future loomed. They hadn't really discussed their relationship beyond the right now but, cheesy as it was, he'd meant what he'd told her at the ball. He'd be her Northern Star. He'd be there for her, if she wanted him. She worked too hard. She needed someone to look out for her best interests.

His heart squeezed. He'd love to be there for her each day, see that smile of hers light up his life like a second sun. Be there for her at night, to cook her dinner and make sure she ate well. Listen to her day and discuss the problems she was dealing with and have her do the same for him.

But his old life in New York still loomed like a specter. All those conferences and lectures and travel he had booked. Long-distance relationships weren't something he'd tried, but from what he'd heard they could be difficult. And perhaps Ayanna wasn't even interested in that with him.

They needed to talk, that much was certain.

As he dictated his surgery notes into the computer, he devised a plan. He'd make her dinner then ask where things stood between them.

"You're quiet tonight," Ayanna said that evening, over a delicious bowl of homemade baked ziti, courtesy of Max's culinary genius. He'd seemed awfully serious since they'd gotten home tonight and it had her on edge. "Everything go okay with the King's surgery?"

"Fine." Max frowned down into his pasta. "How was your day?"

"Good." She tore off another piece of garlic bread and nibbled on the warm crust. Yep, something was definitely off here. Ayanna pressed her knees together under the table and tried not to imagine the worst. The night Will had told her about his affair with Rinna had felt very similar, full of tension and unspoken words. Was she missing something? Was Max leaving sooner than she thought? The King's surgery was done, but she'd expected him to at least stick around until his patient was released. Maybe she'd been wrong. Her stomach cramped and she put the rest of her bread down, uneaten. "Please tell me what's bothering you. I can tell there's a problem."

Max looked up at her then, his eyes stormy. "What's happening here, with us?"

"What do you mean?" Ayanna swallowed hard. "We're enjoying each other's company."

"Is that all?"

"Isn't that enough?"

Max got up to take his plate to the sink and Ayanna's heart sank. She'd apparently said the wrong thing but wasn't sure what. She stood too and moved in beside him at the sink. They bumped arms and Ayanna pulled back. "Sorry. We seem to be in each other's way tonight."

Lips compressed, he looked over at her. "No, I'm sorry. I'm can't seem to find the right way to—"

Her phone buzzed on the table.

Ayanna held up a finger then went back to answer it. On the screen, her mother's face glowed brightly. With a sigh, Ayanna pressed answer, her gaze still locked on Max. "Hey, Mom. What's up?"

"Hi, honey. Just checking on your plans for Christmas," her mother said. "It's less than two weeks away."

"Yes, I know." Ayanna rolled her eyes then turned away from Max, who was still frowning.

"Be sure to invite Max also," her mom said. "You two make such a nice couple and he seemed to really hit it off with everyone."

"We're not a couple, Mom." Ayanna glanced back over her shoulder to see a shadow flicker across his handsome face. Man, something was really wrong, and she had no idea what. The pit in her stomach bottomed out. That old niggle of doubt bored deeper into her gut.

"Hey, Mom. I need to call you back, okay? I'll let you know about Christmas." She hung up before her mother could respond. Max walked past her and into the living room, slumping down on the sofa to stare at the blank TV screen, the glow of the Christmas lights the only other illumination in the room. Feeling like she was walking through a mine-field, Ayanna made her way over to him and sat on the opposite end of the sofa, curling her legs up beneath her, anxiety and apprehension stinging like angry bees inside her. She sensed something precious had been lost, but she couldn't say exactly what yet. "What did you want to tell me before at dinner?"

Max blinked a few times, his expression resigned. "I'm flying back to New York on Christmas Day, pending any unforeseen complications with the King's condition."

"Oh." The news punched her right in the heart. So he was leaving sooner than she'd expected. It should've been fine. Good. She'd known eventually he'd return to his other life across the country, but things had been so happy and idyllic here in Seattle for them the past few weeks she'd allowed herself to get lost in their fantasy bubble.

But all happy bubbles burst eventually, don't they?

Man, how stupid could she have been? She of all people should know that after what had happened with Will. Life had seemed happy and idyllic to her then too, until it hadn't anymore. She had no right to feel surprised or hurt now. Max had been nothing but honest with her from the start. She forced words past the lump of sadness and self-recriminations in her throat. "Okay. Thanks for telling me."

He gave a curt nod. "Figured you should know, even though we aren't a couple or anything."

Red flags went up in her mind and defensiveness joined the ball of whirling emotions inside her. "Do you want us to be a couple?"

Max looked over at her again, his expression unreadable. "Do you?"

Yes. No. I don't know.

She couldn't seem to think straight at the moment. She cared for him deeply, but there were a lot of other factors they needed to discuss that hadn't been factored in when all this was just temporary. What about her job? What about his? Could they make a go of it? Did they even want to try? In the end, she told her truth, "I don't know."

"Right." Max stood and headed for the hall. "I'm going to bed. Got early rounds in the morning."

"Goodnight," she said to his retreating back, her voice as dazed as she felt. Long after he'd gone, Ayanna sat there staring at the tree, wondering how in the world everything had come crashing down so fast.

CHAPTER FOURTEEN

By Christmas Eve morning, things were even more crazy in Ayanna's life, even though the ball was over. The media were still barking at her heels about the accident and the King had woken up after his surgery. She was doing her best to keep the media at bay on both fronts until Dr. di Rossi could make a formal announcement, but it was getting harder by the day.

Then there was Max. Since he'd dropped the bombshell on her about leaving on Christmas Day, to say things between them had been strained would be an understatement. In fact, she hadn't seen Max at all since he'd had the call about the King regaining consciousness in the early hours this morning and had rushed to Seattle General to monitor the King's condition and keep the royal family and Dr. di Rossi updated. She assumed he'd slept there, since she'd woken up alone in bed and there was no sign of his return.

With a sigh, she rolled over and blinked into the darkness. It wasn't yet five. They hadn't made love in almost two weeks. Just kept to their separate sides of the bed, even though every cell in her body had yearned for him. She'd tried to approach him a couple of times, get him to open up and talk, but he'd shut her out, his gray-green gaze as chilly and unreadable as it had been when they'd first met.

Maybe it was for the best. He was leaving and there was no sense in her getting even more attached to him than she already was. She'd known the score going into this and she'd chosen to sleep with him anyway. She'd fallen in love, against her own common sense. If she was miserable now, there was no one to blame but herself.

It was just like the breakup with Will all over again.

She'd blinded herself to the truth then too and look where that had gotten her. Hurt and heartbroken.

Being here in the suite alone gave Ayanna her first taste of what living without Max would be like and it wasn't pleasant. The world felt a bit smaller without him.

Unable to sleep, she finally got up and got ready. Might as well head into work herself. Maybe the busyness of her office would distract her from the pain of losing him. She finished showering and brushing her teeth, then padded into the bedroom to get dressed, clicking on the local morning news in the background while she dressed. According to the weatherman, the temperature had turned chillier and he predicted a chance of light snow later. Perfect. Ayanna chose her black wool designer pantsuit, thinking it would be the warmest choice.

"And in other breaking news…" the anchor said, going to a breaking news story. "We've just learned the identity of this man, seen entering and leaving Seattle General Hospital several times since late November. He's Dr. Maxwell Granger, a world-renowned neurosurgeon whose patient roster includes celebrities and world dignitaries. We haven't yet confirmed the reason for Dr. Granger's appearance here in Seattle, but we speculate it may have something to do with King Roberto of Isola Verde and an auto accident that occurred back on November twenty-first of this year.

"As we reported last month, Dr. Granger visited the royal palace of the wealthy island nation to provide a medial consultation to the King. Our correspondent has reached out to the public relations office for Seattle General Hospital but the facility had no official comment about the accident at this time. They also refused to give any details as to why Dr. Granger was at their hospital, and our attempts to contact Dr. Granger personally have been unsuccessful. We will continue to bring you updates on the late breaking story as they become available. Interestingly…"

Ayanna lowered the volume then sank down on the edge of the bed, dazed. Thank goodness for her intrepid staff. They'd managed to keep a lid on things, though for how long was anyone's guess. She glanced up at the screen again and spotted a picture of Max and a woman she assumed to be his wife, Laura.

Ayanna raised the volume again to hear the anchor say, "…Dr. Granger's skills as a neurosurgeon are well known, yet he was unable to save his own wife, also a physician, who died two years ago from an undiagnosed brain aneurysm. Let's hope King Roberto fares better under Dr. Granger's care."

She shut the TV off then stared down at her toes. Blood rushed in her ears and her ribcage contracted. Max guarded his privacy fiercely and would flip when he saw the news story. It would open up old wounds for him and make things between them even worse. She'd told him she had the situation under control, had bragged to him about how good she was at her job.

This was bad. Very, very bad.

She needed to get to the hospital, and fast, both to talk to Dr. di Rossi and make sure Max was okay. Ayanna hurriedly finished dressing, for once not caring that she had no makeup on, then pulled her damp hair back into a ponytail before shoving her feet into her pumps and grabbing her bag before rushing out the door. By the time she reached the elevators, she was already dialing her office.

Her staff picked up on the second ring. "Did you see the news?"

"Yes." Ayanna headed through the parking garage toward her vehicle, climbing in behind the wheel and starting the engine, switching the call over to Bluetooth as she pulled out of her spot and headed up the ramp to street level. "Please contact Dr. di Rossi and tell him I'll meet him at his office as soon as I get to Seattle General."

"Thank you. Keep the change," Max said to the cashier in the cafeteria after paying for his tea. He'd just finished another neurological check on the King. After a month in a coma and two brain surgeries, both the man's sensory and motor functions had all proved normal as did his reflexes. All in all, Roberto was very lucky, recovering well from both the trauma of the car accident and the removal of his brain tumor.

He took a seat at a small table in a secluded corner and tried to feel better about the fact his case had been a success. Prior to coming to Seattle, that would've been enough. In fact, he would've already been planning ahead for his next patient, his next conference, his next international location.

But after the way his conversation with Ayanna had ended just over a week ago, his heart was heavy. She'd not given him any indication she wanted him to stay in Seattle and if he was smart, he'd take that for what it was—goodbye. Except for some reason he couldn't. Even knowing she didn't want a relationship with him, even knowing it would never work between them, he hated the thought of leaving her. He loved Ayanna, but sometimes love wasn't enough. Look at what had happened with him and Laura.

Wincing, he swallowed more of his hot tea, glad of the distracting scald on the back of his throat, then sighed, staring down at his wrinkled scrubs. The best thing for everyone would be for him to get showered and changed, clear his head and look at this situation logically, analytically, without his blasted heart getting in the way and mucking it all up. The King's next check wasn't for another couple of hours and he'd already been removed from the consult rotation for the ER, pending his departure tomorrow, so he had nothing but time on his hands at the moment.

Time and regret.

His heart pinched and his stomach dropped, along with his spirits.

People came and went from the tables around him, but Max barely noticed. Restless, he glanced up at the TV mounted on the wall nearby. The local morning news was on, but the volume was off. Closed captioning across the bottom showed what the anchor was saying. For a moment the image on the screen didn't register. Then he blinked and squinted, disbelief overriding the shadows inside him. That was him, his picture beside the King's. His body tensed. Ayanna and her staff had worked day and night to keep the King's accident and surgery out of the media. She must be frantic right now.

Then another photo popped up on the screen of him and Laura and his concern for Ayanna quickly morphed into outrage. With the types of patients he treated, Max was no stranger to paparazzi, but how dared they invade his privacy? What gutted him the most, though, were the words scrolling across the bottom of the screen, "…he was unable to save his own wife…"

Guilt that had eased during his weeks here with Ayanna returned hot and heavy in his torso, expanding to fill his extremities. This was exactly why it was better not to feel anything. Because once you opened up the floodgates it all came in, the good and the bad. His breath shallow, he threw away the rest of his tea and headed back to the relative privacy of the ICU, jaw tense and skin too tight for his body. As he stalked through the walkways and halls then took the stairs to the third floor, he couldn't stop berating himself for being such an idiot. He'd learned his lesson growing up—emotions got you nothing but trouble. He should have come here, done his job, then got out. No fuss, no muss, no mess.

We're not a couple.

Ayanna's words to her mother on the phone on the night of the King's surgery haunted him once more and he gave a derisive snort. Good thing he hadn't asked her to start a relationship with him, a real one, told her he'd loved her, even if it currently felt like he'd taken a bullet straight to the heart. The best thing for both of them was to end things now, cleanly, and go back to the lives waiting for them. End of story.

He pushed out of the stairwell and into the ICU, running a hand through his hair. At the other end of the hall, where the King's room was located, he spotted Ayanna and Dr. di Rossi emerging from Roberto's room. Neither of them noticed him approach as they were deep in conversation, but Max cleared his throat, making his presence known.

Dr. di Rossi extended his hand, leaning in so Ayanna wouldn't hear him. "Thank you, Max, for everything you've done for my father. My family is forever in your debt. Now, if you'll excuse me, I have something urgent to do…"

Once he'd gone, Ayanna led Max into a small private conference room, looking as unhappy as he felt. "I take it you saw the news story."

"I did. It's fine," he said, even though it really wasn't. He couldn't seem to stand still, pacing the small space to diffuse some of the nervous energy rioting through him. Too bad he couldn't seem to flip that switch and turn off his emotions, like he had in the past.

"It's not fine," Ayanna said. "The media needs to stop. This is what I do for a living, Max. I've already spoken to Dr. di Rossi about the King's story in all this. Let me do some damage control for you too and—"

"Damage control?" He gave an unpleasant laugh and shook his head. "God. Is that what these past few weeks together have come to? I thought…" His scowl deepened. "Never mind. It doesn't matter what I thought."

"Max, I'm sorry. I shouldn't have put it like that." The hurt in her eyes made him feel worse, if that were possible. "It's just a turn of phrase. It doesn't mean anything."

"And there's the problem, in a nutshell. None of this really means anything, does it? The time we spent together, making love. It was all just a temporary affair. We go our separate ways and get back to our separate lives."

"Hey. We both knew this was a fling, right? Besides, you're the one leaving tomorrow for New York. Not me." She took a deep breath, her posture as stiff as a board and the toe of her pump tapping soundlessly on the beige carpet. "Look, we're both tired and under a lot of stress. If you've got something to say about us, then say it. I can't read between your lines all the time and guess whatever it is you're feeling. Sorry. I've been there, done that, and don't plan on taking that trip again."

"You want to know what I'm feeling?" he asked. Max struggled to keep his voice down, hating that his anger and frustration were ruling him but unable to tamp them down. "I'm feeling like an idiot. Like this whole affair between us was nothing but a mistake. I let you in, Ayanna, I opened up to you, but I shouldn't have. Because the truth is I'm not available. My work doesn't allow me the time or emotional space for other people in my life. I'm alone for a reason."

"What a load of crap." Ayanna inched closer, her eyes bright with fury. "You know what I think? I think what you're feeling is scared. Scared of your emotions. Scared of taking a chance with me because the truth is that love terrifies you. Well, guess what, mister big-time surgeon. That's the name of the game. Love is scary. It's messy and maddening and magnificent. But you'll never let yourself have that again because you've already closed yourself off again in that tight shell of yours."

"Like you're one to talk." He inched closer to Ayanna as well, crossing a line in the proverbial sand but unable to stop now. "You're scared too. Scared to be less than perfect. Scared to trust yourself and make another mistake. Scared that if you can't be everything to everybody all the time, no one will ever love you."

Her face turned ashen and her mouth opened wordlessly. Yeah, he'd gone too far. He wanted nothing more than to take his hateful words back, but it was too late. They hung in the air, potent and poisonous, eating away at whatever possibilities might have been left between them like acid on metal.

"We're done here," Ayanna finally managed to say, her tone brittle. "Have a nice trip home, Dr. Granger. I'll head back to the suite now to pack my things and disappear from your life forever. Merry Christmas."

Max stared at the door after she walked out, unable to move. He was alone again, just as he'd wanted. Except the gaping black hole where his heart should've been didn't feel like what he wanted at all. He slumped down into a nearby chair and dropped his head into his hands, desperately wishing for the icy monotony of his old façade while fearing it—along with Ayanna—was gone for good.

CHAPTER FIFTEEN

AYANNA HAD RUSHED back to the hotel after leaving Max, shoved things into her bags as quickly as she could then returned to Seattle General. Now, hours later, she sat in her office, trying to finish up some last-minute things before leaving for the holiday and not think about the horrible fight with Max. Funny, but when the breakup with Will had occurred, there'd been no fireworks, no shouting or arguments. She'd been too shocked and Will hadn't cared enough at that point to fight.

If that didn't prove how much she loved Max, Ayanna didn't know what did.

Not that it mattered. He'd be gone soon and she'd be left here to pick up the pieces and go on. Same as always. Chalk up another failure for her stupid instincts.

With a sigh, she closed her eyes and once again her mind replayed their argument.

What he'd said about her need for perfection, about her trust issues, about her fearing no one would love her if she didn't take care of them had been hitting below the belt. Trouble was, they also happened to be true.

Darn it.

She hated admitting that, but there it was. Max had always been far too perceptive for his own good. He also happened to know her better than anyone else, even in the short time they'd been together. He got her, more than her parents, more than her family. Way more than Will ever had.

Max was her person. She loved him.

And now he was leaving.

Because I pushed him away.

A knock sounded at the door and one of her staffers, a young intern named Gretchen, popped her head inside, a pair of glittery reindeer antlers on her head. "Hey, boss. Staff party's wrapping up and I wanted to wish you Happy Holidays before I go."

"Thank you." Ayanna forced a smile. "I hope you have a wonderful holiday too, Gretchen."

"Thanks, boss." Gretchen raised a glass of eggnog. "You sure you don't want to take a break and join us? We're probably going to hit the pub down the street after we leave here."

"Aw, thank you for the invitation, but no." Ayanna shook her head. "I'm pretty tired. You guys have fun and be careful. No drinking and driving, all right?"

"Yes, ma'am." Gretchen saluted. "See you in the new year."

"See you." She waited until the office emptied then tried again to get through the stack of papers that hadn't budged since she'd first sat down earlier this afternoon, but it was hopeless.

She covered her face with her hands and slumped back in her seat. God, she'd really messed things up with Max. He had a right to feel however he wanted to feel about the media invading his privacy and his wife's death. She should have supported his decision, whatever it was, and helped him through it, not berated him about it. Man, some PR expert she was.

Sniffling, Ayanna yanked a tissue from the box on her desk. They hadn't been apart a full day yet and already she missed him. Her first instinct was to go to his office down the hall, but he wasn't there anymore. She'd peeked down the hall when she'd returned from the hotel and it looked like he'd already cleared out the space. And speaking of clearing out, she needed to call her parents about staying at their place next week since the suite wasn't an option anymore and the work on her apartment still wasn't finished.

Looked like she'd end up back in her old room after all. She was going to be there tomorrow for Christmas anyway, so it made sense. With a sigh, she picked up her phone and texted her mother.

Mind if I come early and spend the night tonight? I'll stay through next week too, if it's okay.

The response came through quicker than she'd expected.

Oh, no! What happened?

Light snow fell as Ayanna walked across the street to the parking lot alone, the sadness in her heart in direct contrast to the jolly decorations lighting up the city around her. Her thumb trembled slightly as she texted back.

I'll explain later. See you soon.

Late that night, Max was back in the hospital cafeteria. The place was all but deserted now because it was Christmas Eve. He should go back to the hotel to sleep, but he just couldn't. Couldn't face being in the suite without Ayanna. Especially knowing he'd basically destroyed any chance he'd had with her.

God, once again his emotions had cost him dearly. He rubbed his hands over his face then stared out the window at the snowy landscape. It was probably good he was leaving tomorrow. After their awful argument, Ayanna would want nothing to do with him and now that the King was on the mend, there was no reason for him to stay.

He stared down into another cup of tea, this one as cold as ice because it had sat there so long. But instead of seeing the beverage, replays of their time together unspooled in his head.

During the few brief weeks they'd shared, Ayanna had shown him a different way to be—happy, carefree, fun. Sure, he'd still had his work and his obligations to his patients, but the burden of guilt he'd carried so long over his wife's death had lifted. He had Ayanna to thank for that. She'd got him talking about it, got it out in the open and helped him release it. She'd been right today too. He'd been using his busy schedule as a shield against being vulnerable and getting hurt again. But instead of protecting him, keeping everyone away had only caused him more pain in the end.

Max sat back and scratched the stubble on his jaw, exhausted but unable to sleep.

He'd mucked things up in the worst way. He should never have poked Ayanna's most painful spots. Why did he have to bring up her ex? Why did he have to push the buttons he knew hurt her most? Why couldn't he have just told her he loved her and wanted to spend the rest of his life with her? Maybe if he had, she'd still be here, and the future ahead of him now wouldn't seem as cold and lonely as the Arctic tundra.

CHAPTER SIXTEEN

ON CHRISTMAS MORNING at her parents' house Ayanna got the grilling she'd expected from her family.

"Spill it, sis," her sister LaTasha said over a batch of their mom's superb cinnamon buns. "I can tell something's wrong."

"How?" Ayanna scowled from across the breakfast bar. "Nothing's wrong."

Five incredulous stares met Ayanna's gaze, along with several raised brows.

Maybe she was sitting here with her hair all ratty and uncombed, not a touch of makeup on and her PJs wrinkled. Couldn't a girl just relax without getting the fifth degree? Apparently not, where her family was concerned. "Okay. Fine. Max and I had an argument yesterday at work."

"Oh, no. Was it about that news story? I saw that; they were harsh about his past,"

James said, giving her a look. "That's none of their business."

"Agreed." Ayanna took a bigger bite than necessary of her roll, not even caring about the crumbs on the front of her shirt. Forget all her fussy perfectionism. She was going full-out mess for a change.

"Sweetie," Tonya, said, handing her a napkin. "Have you tried calling him? Maybe you can still work things out. Max seemed pretty great to me."

Talking about her problems with her siblings wasn't exactly comfortable for Ayanna. In fact, it was downright embarrassing. She was the oldest, the one who was supposed to have it all together. The one who took care of everyone else. But no longer. That was the old her. The her that had driven Max away.

The new her was all about letting it all hang out—mistakes and mussiness and all.

Scared that if you can't be everything to everybody all the time, no one will ever love you...

Max's words looped through her head. Yep. That extreme hadn't worked for her at all. Maybe this other one would. She took a sip of her peppermint tea, the tips of her ears hot as her siblings continued to eyeball her as if she were an alien life form who'd invaded Ayanna's body.

Tonya was right. Max was great. One of the best men she'd ever met. And now he was gone. Loneliness clawed inside her, making her grip her mug tighter. She missed him, so much it ached. She'd not slept a wink last night. Just stared up at the ceiling in her old room and remembered when she and Max had stood in there together on Thanksgiving.

Tears stung her eyes before she could blink them away, all her love for him swamping her at once and drowning her in a whirlpool of sadness. Great, now she could add red and puffy to her growing list of new looks she'd tried.

"Aw, sweetie." Her family gathered around her in a group hug that included her mom and dad. "Don't cry."

Another great thing about families. They always had your back, no matter how you screwed up.

Minutes later, after more hugs and tears, Ayanna blew her nose, then frowned down at her cold tea. "I pushed Max away because I couldn't trust myself and what I was feeling after what happened with Will, and now I've lost him."

"Oh, honey." Her mom rubbed her back.

"Don't give up so easy. If I hadn't stuck it out with your dad when we were dating, we never would've ended up together. Believe me, he was not easy to be around all the time. Moody and brooding and then he went and dated another woman behind my back and—"

"Hey!" Her father gave her mom a look. "I didn't date that woman. We went out one time to make you jealous, Nari. Worked too, since you wouldn't leave me alone after that."

"Hush." Her mom tossed a balled-up napkin at his head. Her dad ducked then chuckled, winking at his wife with obvious affection. "Don't listen to him. He pursued me like the queen I am and that's why we got back together. Listen, honey. Will wasn't worth your time. You were always too good for him. But Max? Now, there's a man who appreciates a good woman. The fact he still feels guilty over his late wife is proof of that. What you need to do now is show him what the future for you two could be like. Men are visual creatures. Show him a new path forward." She pushed Ayanna's hair behind her ear then kissed her temple. "But whatever you do, honey, do it fast. Time's aticking."

Ayanna glanced at the clock then picked up her phone. It was ten o'clock now. Max's flight was this afternoon. If she hurried, she might be able to catch him at the airport before he left. She knew what she wanted. Max. Pure and simple. Exactly how they'd make it work she wasn't sure, but, man, she wanted to try.

Determination fluttered inside her and she straightened, pushing aside her cold tea. "I'm going to get him."

"About damned time," her mother said, slipping her arm around her husband's waist. "Might want to take a shower first, though."

Max stood on the porch of Ayanna's parents' house late the next morning, wondering when exactly he'd lost his mind. He hadn't slept more than an hour the night before and felt even more tired now. Tired and empty. He'd never felt so empty before. Not after his parents had died. Not after losing Laura.

It was like there was a huge, gaping, Ayanna-sized hole inside him and the only cure was inside the house before him. But whether or not he could ever get her back was another question. Exhaling slowly, he gripped the handle of the wheeled suitcase beside him and glanced back over his shoulder at the cab still idling at the curb. His flight didn't leave for a few more hours, but he'd checked out of the hotel anyway, thinking he'd head to the airport early. Nothing to keep him in Seattle now. Nothing but all the memories, all the regrets. For the first time in a long time he had nowhere to be. He was adrift and he didn't like it.

He stared at the candy cane wreath on the front door of her parents' house again, its cheerful bright red bow mocking him. Maybe he should just leave and go back to Manhattan, get back into his routine. That usually made him feel better.

Except there was nothing waiting for him in New York either. Nothing except another empty room.

Until he'd come here, he'd never had a problem being alone, but now everything had changed. Because of Ayanna. The woman he loved and had driven away.

To add insult to injury, the head of neurosurgery had stopped him on his way out of the hospital last night and offered him a permanent position on their staff. They'd even been willing to work around Max's hectic travel schedule, since his reputation and expertise would bring in many more high-profile clients to Seattle General. He'd seriously considered it for a moment—the constant travel and work that had driven him the past two years had grown old—but staying in the city now would mean constantly wondering if he might see Ayanna around the next corner. It would've been too painful.

In his mind, scenes from *It's a Wonderful Life* played like a sign from above. What Max wouldn't do for a little angelic intervention right about now.

You see, you've really had a wonderful life. What a mistake it would be to throw it away...

Clarence the angel had said that line to George Bailey in the movie, but to Max now it sounded like it was meant just for him. Life here in Seattle these past few weeks with Ayanna had been pretty wonderful. In fact, she'd made every one of his days brighter just by being there. She'd made him feel like he could climb any mountain, solve any case, be a better man.

And if that wasn't a heavenly gift, and the best Christmas present ever, Max didn't know what was.

Before he could rethink his actions, he pulled out his cellphone to change his flight. There was every chance in the world Ayanna might tell him to get lost, but that was a chance he was willing to take. He'd open his battered heart and be vulnerable, if it meant he might get to spend forever with the woman he loved.

After switching to a later return, after the new year, Max signaled to the cab driver to continue waiting then faced the door of Ayanna's parents' house once more. He rang the bell then glanced upward to the porch roof, saying, "Thanks, Clarence. Wish me luck."

CHAPTER SEVENTEEN

"HURRY BACK, HONEY," Ayanna's mom said. "There's dinner later and I've got so much food. Plus presents."

"I know, Mom. With luck I'll get to SeaTac before his flight leaves." Ayanna tugged her coat on over the jeans and sweatshirt she'd changed into after her shower, her damp hair pulled back into a ponytail, no makeup. She leaned over to peck her mom's cheek on her way to the foyer. "I don't want to miss Max again."

"Fine. But after you find that man of yours, drag him straight back here to eat, you hear me?" The huge ham her mom had been cooking all night in the kitchen had the house smelling like cloves and cinnamon.

"Will do. Mom." Ayanna grabbed her bag.

"You got love in your heart, honey. That's all the luck you need."

Ayanna had just reached for the door

handle when the bell rang. Thinking it was David, James's partner, Ayanna opened it up to dash past the guy, only to find Max standing there, looking disheveled and distraught and decidedly delicious.

He stared at her, his cheeks pink from the cold, wariness and surprise warring in his gray-green eyes. "Uh, hey." Max said at last. "Merry Christmas."

"Who is it, sis?" LaTasha asked, moving in beside Ayanna. "Oh!"

"Is that David?" James traipsed up next, his stockinged feet pounding across the hardwood, his attention focused on his phone and not the person at the door. "He'd better have an excuse for being late, and—"

Her brother looked up and stopped in midrant, wide-eyed. James recovered faster than his sisters, though, and nudged Ayanna's ribs. "Girl, go get him."

"Hey, James," Max said, his small smile cautious. "I came to talk to Ayanna."

"Good." James reached past a still frozen Ayanna and tugged Max inside before herding them both into a small library across the foyer. "Whatever's going on with you two, work it out." He started to close the door, leaving them in privacy. "Kiss and make up already."

Alone with Max, Ayanna felt even more tongue-tied and twisted. They looked anywhere but at each other and her cheeks burned hotter than the surface of the sun.

Just tell him, girl. Trust yourself.

"I...uh..." she started, finding it hard to say what she needed with him actually standing there in front of her. Ayanna took a deep breath then forced herself to continue. Now or never. "I'm sorry about what I said during our argument. I was wrong,"

"No, you were right," Max said. "And I'm the one who's sorry. I have been using my work as a shield." He stepped forward and took her hand. "But unless I change and let you in, I'll be alone forever and that's not what I want."

A small tree glowed in the corner of the room, casting them in flickering shades of red and green and blue. Ayanna squeezed his fingers. "You were right too. I was scared to make mistakes, scared to trust myself and what I was feeling." She looked up at him, meeting his gaze with her tear-filled eyes. "But I'm not scared anymore. Because I love you, Max."

"I love you too, Ayanna." Max stepped closer, the heat of him warming her heart.

"I want to make a new life with you, here in Seattle, if you'll have me."

He kissed her gently and her breath hitched. It was the sweetest, most wonderful present she ever could have asked for, but there was still one small doubt left in Ayanna's mind. "But what about your life in New York? What about your career there?"

"My career is wherever my patients are. And my life is with you, Ayanna. I can travel anywhere, if need be, but the head of neurosurgery at Seattle General offered me a position on staff last night and I'm going to take it. This place already feels more like more of a home to me than New York ever did, thanks to you."

A scuffle sounded on the other side of the library door and Ayanna chuckled. "I think my family's listening in."

"I think you're right." He chuckled then kissed her again, this time more deeply, wrapping his arms around her and holding her close. "No matter where I go, Ayanna, I'll always come back to you."

"Same." She pulled him down for another kiss until whoops and hollers echoing from the foyer beyond had them pulling apart again, laughing. "We can share my apartment for a while, maybe save up for a house together."

"Sounds perfect," he said, smiling. "Did I mention that I love you, Ayanna Franklin?"

"Yes, you did, Max Granger." She rose up on tiptoe to kiss him again. "And I love you too."

Then the door opened and her mom stuck her head in. "Now that everyone loves everyone else again, you two get out here and help me with all this food. We've got a Christmas to celebrate."

"C'mon, lovebirds," Tonya said, waving them out. "I want to open my gifts now."

"Me too!" LaTasha chimed in. "Girl, you better have gotten me that book I wanted."

"Since when do you read?" James snorted, shepherding everyone down the hall to the dining room where Brandon, Clarissa and their dad were busy setting the table. He checked his phone again then announced. "David is on his way. And, Tasha, the last thing you read was the back of the box for that dye that turned your hair green. You better get your butt into my salon soon so I can fix that before it all falls out."

"I liked my green hair. Makes me feel like a mermaid," Ayanna's sister said. "At least I have hair. You tell people you shaved your head, but I know the truth."

Gasps and laughter broke out from the group and then her parents got involved and things rapidly deteriorated from there. From the relative quiet of the doorway, Ayanna shook her head then hazarded a glance up at Max, his hand still in hers, just the way she hoped it would always be. "You sure you want to join this crazy family?"

"As long as you're in it…" Max looked down at her, his smile brimming with joy "…absolutely."

* * * * *